Dig Two Graves

Detective Solomon Gray, Volume 1

Keith Nixon

Published by Gladius Press, 2019.

Other Novels by Keith Nixon

One

A door slammed somewhere down the hall, and a drunk shouted in the corridor before a copper shut him up. Inside interview room three, Solomon Gray ignored it all.

Carslake scraped his chair as he drew himself up to the table. Harder to do these days as his waist was expanding. He had a soft face, but Gray knew better than to underestimate him.

Carslake said something; to Gray it was just white noise.

Gray looked up at the crack in the Artex ceiling where the pipe had burst last year. A blob of water hung from a brown stain. He watched as a drop hit the table.

There was the strike of a lighter, the flare of a flame, the crackle of Carslake's first drag. "Want a smoke, Sol?"

"I want my son back." Gray was bereft of sentiment, his mind trapped in the shock phase of the grief cycle. He felt nothing.

The lighter flickered once more. It was Fowler this time, his porn-star moustache stained with nicotine. "Go on," he said, yellow teeth exposed in a grin as he held out a glowing cigarette. "Take it." Fowler was always one to provide temptation.

Gray didn't have the strength to argue. The smoke burst into his lungs, opened the airways. It made him feel light-headed. He wished he hadn't accepted Fowler's offer now.

"Have you made your call?" asked Carslake.

Gray nodded. "Reverend Hill is on his way to tell Kate. Alice is going with him."

His wife, Kate. How was she going to deal with this?

"Wise," said Carslake. *In other words*, Gray thought, *someone else's problem right now*. Carslake had bigger fish to fry. "Is the recorder running?"

"Yep, started it a minute ago," said Fowler.

Carslake took another drag on the cigarette, the ember a bright spark in the dimly lit room, then let a sigh escape in a plume of smoke.

"This is an interview with Detective Sergeant Solomon Gray. Present are Detective Constable Michael Fowler and Detective Sergeant Jeffrey Carslake. Time is...7:35 p.m. on the 15th of December, 2006."

7:35 p.m.? Was that all? It felt like it should be much later.

Carslake rested his forearms on the battered table between them. They'd all pulled a full shift and then some. The weight of the day and friction of the job lingered like Fowler's body odour.

Carslake loosened his tie, beads of sweat forming on his brow. The space was small, and the radiator against the far wall couldn't be turned down, the valve broken and awaiting repair.

"What happened, Sol?" said Carslake, his voice indulgent.

"I took Tom to the fair. It's his birthday."

"We know that," said Fowler. "Tell us something new."

Gray paused. New? To him this was all new. A unique emotion, perhaps the last he would ever feel. Carslake glared at Fowler, who held his hands up in surrender.

"Carry on, Sol."

"I took Tom to the fair. It's his birthday," repeated Gray, his memory organised in a straight line.

"Just the two of you?"

A sharp nod. "The original plan was we'd go as a family, but Hope wasn't feeling too well so Kate stayed behind. We were all disappointed. Hope's only two years older and it would have been great fun for her, too."

"How old is Tom?" Carslake knew the answer. It was for the tape.

"Six. He's six. And he's out there somewhere alone."

Gray rose from his seat, driven to start looking for his son again. Carslake placed a restraining hand on his arm.

"Sit down. We've got all boots on the ground right now. Understand?" After a moment, Gray nodded and settled again. "Good. Now, what was the fair like?"

Gray skipped back a few hours in his mind. Bright lights, screams of enjoyment, loud music. "You know how they are. Seen one, you've seen them all." Gray shrugged, stubbed out the cigarette.

"Go on," prompted Carslake.

"I came home late. Shift overran."

"When doesn't it?"

"True." Gray tried to laugh, but it sounded more like a wheeze. "Kate was angry about it. Reminded me it was Tom's birthday. The local kids had been and gone, the presents opened and played with, the cake cut and demolished. She told me, 'The one thing you had to do was get home on time.'"

"What did you say?"

"The same as every other working father."

Carslake shrugged. "Why don't you just tell me?"

"I have to work to pay the bills. No job, no money. Rough with the smooth, you know?"

"I bet that went down well."

Gray grimaced. "No."

"And then?"

"I didn't even get changed. I took Tom straight out. Kate didn't thank me; she clearly thought it was the least I could do. Tom was delighted, though." Gray smiled. His penultimate happy memory. The pleasure dropped away almost instantly. It felt inappropriate.

"We won a few things on the stalls. Went on a couple of rides." Gray remembered sitting on a roundabout and then some swings.

"Did you hit the dodgems?" asked Fowler. "They're great fun. First thing I head for." Tom had shrieked with delight when they were thumped into by another dodgem.

Carslake furrowed his brow at Fowler. "Keep going, Sol."

"Tom had been nagging me all evening about the ghost train. But we'd left the house in a rush and I hadn't picked up my wallet so I was short of cash. In the end, I folded. I told Tom it would be the last thing we'd do, then it was home time. I was knackered."

"So, you went to the ghost train..." nudged Carslake.

"I tried to get out of it one last time by saying we were short of money, that we both couldn't ride, but..."

He choked, a moan catching in his throat. The other two detectives waited for Gray to compose himself.

"Tom was so keen he said he'd go by himself. I had two choices. I could take him home, kicking and screaming, and face Kate's wrath or... you know."

"You let him go on?" said Fowler, unable to keep the disbelief out of his voice. "The lad's six years old."

"If I could go back and change it, believe me, I would."

"There's no need to justify yourself," said Carslake. "What happened after that?"

"We queued. Tom held my hand the whole time. I could feel him trembling with excitement. The car arrived. He sat down, and he looked so small that I almost stopped him there and then. Then the bar dropped down and off he went, into the darkness, a huge grin on his face." Gray stared into the middle distance. "He didn't come out again."

"What do you mean?"

"When his carriage came back, it was empty."

"What did you do?"

"I just stood there. Then I dropped everything I was holding and pushed inside. It was dark. I fumbled around, couldn't find anyone. Not even the ghost. I shouted for Tom. No reply. I ran out behind the ride. Nothing. It was as if he'd vanished into thin air."

"And then?"

A heartbeat, another. "I screamed."

Two

Ten Years Later

Death was often pointless, but, given the circumstances, a plummet of five floors from balcony to roadside was at the extreme end of the spectrum.

Detective Sergeant Solomon Gray was surrounded by white. Powerful lights blazed over the scene, the beams reflecting off the canvas tent sides erected to shield the body from the elements and preserve any evidence.

The jumper was young, a boy on the cusp of manhood. When Gray first caught sight of the corpse, that same shock arced through him like it always did whenever a report came in about a child in trouble or worse, dead. Could it be his Tom? He squatted down to take a closer look. No, this one was older. Relief, then – hot on its heels – guilt. Once more he'd avoided facing up to reality.

What the hell drove someone with their whole life ahead of them into a swan dive with only one possible outcome?

Suicide cases. He hated them.

According to an eyewitness, the kid had screamed all the way down. A natural response? Or had he changed his mind when it was too late? Or maybe he was unwilling to jump in the first place?

The kid looked remarkably peaceful, given that one side of his body was smashed into the pavement. Gravity and concrete had fashioned him into a chaotic canvas, an abstract that wouldn't look out of place in the recently built art museum less than a mile away. If it wasn't for the Jackson Pollock blood splatter and the vacant, staring eyes, Gray could have imagined him asleep.

Gray's mind was like an artist's palette, assumptions and suppositions whirling into one colourful mess. The past joining with the present. A reminder of his wife's passing. By her own hand, too.

"Are you all right?" asked the attending pathologist, Dr Ben Clough, who loomed over Gray, casting a long shadow. He peered at Gray through his glasses with unblinking eyes. Clough was a neat, precise man. Combed sandy hair, trimmed fingernails, washed clothes. The antithesis of Gray in appearance, identical to Gray in the difficulty he had connecting with people. Clough was competent bordering on arrogant.

Clough had the wiry physique of an athlete, all sinew and muscle. When not working ridiculously long hours he pounded the streets, loping mile after mile. Most presumed it was an escape from his job. Gray knew Clough just preferred solitude. He could relate to that.

"I've seen everything I need to," said Gray.

"Haven't we all." Clough sounded much older than he looked. "I'll call when the post-mortem is scheduled."

The pair exchanged brief farewells out of courtesy before Gray gratefully stepped out of the evidence tent.

It was overcast and chilly outside. Arlington House, a granite-grey high-rise on the Margate seafront and the deceased's diving board, was perfectly in keeping with the seasonal inclemency and the dingy atmosphere. It looked like a monumental tomb. Gray counted five floors and fixed his eyes on the offending balcony. It didn't look that high up. He wiped a hand over his forehead. It came away slick.

A gust of wind slapped Gray; reminded him it was December, when autumn was buried and past, and winter was tightening its grip. Christmas was on the way, which meant impending merriment, a holiday and, worst of all, the anniversary of Tom's disappearance.

A crowd of onlookers had continued to grow while he was talking with the good doctor. They pressed against the cordon, eager to catch a glimpse of the tragedy. Those nearest the tent flap craned their necks, flamingo-like, teetering on tiptoes to see inside. Then the flash of a camera.

Gray felt like hunting down the snapper and ramming the lens where it wouldn't be found. What was it with people? Why did they take such pleasure in witnessing the misfortune of others? Like rubber neckers on a motorway, scoping out the scene of an accident. Morbid bastards with their misplaced invincibility, their unwavering belief that such a fate could never happen to them, that their deaths would come quietly, peacefully in old, old age.

Gray knew better.

He'd been around long enough to recognise trouble when he saw it. Soon the jostling for a better look would turn to shoving, then a scuffle, a couple of arrests, followed by paperwork he could do without. Hours of police time squandered. The magistrate would no doubt issue little more than a caution to the offenders after a night in the cells. All of it due to the pursuit of momentary gory gratification. A tinderbox of misfortune that just needed a spark.

And there it was. Ed Scully, a ruddy-faced freelance newspaper reporter and general ne'er-do-well. Scully was as slick as engine oil, a chameleon who changed his appearance at will to blend with the crowd. Today he was dressed down in jeans and a jacket zipped up to the neck. His hair was shaved back to the skull. If there was bad news, Scully could always be found trailing in its wake, like a seagull following a trawler, scavenging the scraps.

There was history between them. The purported journalist had cut his teeth on Gray's misfortunes and continued to nip at him every chance he got. Scully never allowed Gray's wounds to heal, pulling up the past and dragging it through the papers, always revealing some detail he shouldn't have known.

Scully oozed through the crowd, seeking prime candidates to interview, those who would deliver the most abhorrent of quotes and so provide the best copy.

Scully's roving eyes spotted Gray. The reporter smiled, then winked. Who better to provide a comment than the harried DS? Gray didn't react beyond an internal tightening of the gut and a clench of his right fist.

He broke eye contact with the hack before Scully could force his way through the squeeze of bodies. There was work to be done and Gray didn't trust himself not to screw it up by slamming his fist into Scully's face.

Gray turned to the grim-faced police constable supervising the cordon. He nodded as the PC lifted the tape and granted him a quick exit. Gray could feel Scully's eyes boring into his spine as he walked on.

A minute or two later, within the relative peace of Arlington House, Gray nudged the up arrow a couple of times to summon the lift. His thumb successfully cajoled the mechanism into a lumbering descent of many floors, if the distant racket was anything to go by. He leant his forehead on the metal doors to cool his sweating brow.

Eventually the lift arrived and Gray stepped back. The doors slowly parted in a *ta-dah!* movement. The lift was empty.

He rattled the same thumb at the number he wanted until the doors closed. He read the graffiti as a distraction from the all-pervasive odour of urine and cigarettes.

The victim's flat was just around the corner from the lift. Gray wouldn't be surprised if the machinery could be heard day and night. The front door leant drunkenly against the corridor wall. Bent hinges, splintered wood, and some black boot marks said it had been kicked down to gain entrance. Gray wondered whether the act was one of benevolence or opportunism. The corridor was suspiciously empty. Not a good sign.

At the entrance, Gray accepted a pair of blue overshoes from a fully kitted out Scenes of Crime Officer and slipped them on, swaying as he did so, stubbornly refusing to put a hand out to steady himself. One foot, then the other. He removed his coat and replaced it with white overalls. He pulled the hood up over his greying hair. Once he put on a face mask, and a pair of latex gloves which obscured nibbled nails and torn cuticles, he was good to go.

Inside was a hive of practised activity. Forensics mingled with CID as they swept the flat for evidence. The party was in the living room, at the end of the corridor which sliced through the flat like an ambulatory highway, off which there were doors to a bathroom, a tiny kitchen, and two bedrooms.

He paused on the threshold for a moment, glanced around.

The interior smelled damp. There were lingering brown stains where the ceiling met the wall, a green bloom of mould in the corners. The furniture, what little there was, was shabby and worn. Light came in through a pair of grimy full-length glass doors that opened onto a precariously narrow balcony.

The only CID presence came in the form of the underfed detective constable, newly shunted over from uniform. The DC was in conversation with a SOCO in front of the balcony. Gray interrupted, ignoring the SOCO's impotent glare: "Where's DI Hamson?"

Detective Inspector Yvonne Hamson was Gray's long-suffering boss, the one who had to put up with all his quirks because nobody else would. She'd be the Senior Investigating Officer.

"In one of the bedrooms, sir."

"Point me in the right direction."

"DS Fowler said I was to find him first when you eventually turned up. His words, sir, not mine."

"Okay then, get him for me instead."

"Sir."

"Hang on," Gray put a restraining hand on the DC's arm, "are our people going door-to-door?"

"Not yet."

"Get them bloody moving, then. Find out if anyone saw or heard anything."

"Yes, sir." The DC's eyes spoke volumes: it was a futile gesture. There would be no witnesses, no statements, no helpful off-the-record tips. There never were. And although Gray knew that was the case, due process, even if it had the relative value of a flatulent bowel movement, must be followed.

Needled by the continued presence of the SOCO, Gray turned and barked, "Haven't you got work to do?" The SOCO moved away without comment. "Thought he'd never clear off."

"He was a she, sir."

"Really?" Gray shrugged, unaffected by the faux pas. "It's hard to tell who's who in these gimp suits."

The DC skedaddled, returning quickly with his man. Thankless mission accomplished, the DC drifted away, exiting the discussion.

Detective Sergeant Mike Fowler was medium everything – height, build, and looks – but possessed a sharp brain, a quick mouth, and a tendency to speak bluntly with often intentional side effects. Fowler was one of those guys who was perfectly happy to censure, but hated the tables being turned.

"How's it going, Mike?" Of the two men, Gray was senior, a time-served thing, and a state of affairs which rubbed Fowler up the wrong way.

"We've only just started. So far it looks like Piccadilly Circus. SOCO turned up a load of fingerprints."

"How many?"

"Dozens, apparently."

"They could have had a party, I suppose," said Gray, which elicited a shrug from Fowler. "What else?"

"A couple of bedrooms, neither in a particularly pristine state."

"Anything major turned up?"

"Depends whether you count mistletoe as evidence of the century or not."

"Mistletoe?"

"Right in the middle of the floor." Fowler pointed at the psychedelic carpet.

Gray didn't know what to make of it. "Is that all?"

"No." Fowler held up three fingers, ticked them off one by one. "Traces of what looks to be cocaine." He indicated a glass-topped table from a bygone era. It was covered in fingerprint dust.

Number two. "A suicide note. Weighed the letter down with a glass so it wouldn't blow away when the balcony door was opened."

"Now there's preparation for you. Where is it?"

Fowler disappeared briefly to find the evidence. Gray glanced out the balcony window; saw brown sea and grey sky. He wasn't a fan of heights so this was as close to the balcony as he'd go.

Fowler returned with a single sheet of A4 in a clear plastic bag. It would have been photographed in situ before being bagged and sealed. The jagged edge along the top of the sheet led Gray to think it had been torn from a pad.

It took Gray a few moments to decipher the shaky scrawl. Fowler was incorrect. There was no justification in the letter, simply a statement of intent. A desire to end it all expressed via a handful of dashed off words and signed *Nick*.

Probably tears, was all Gray could think when he reached the final full stop, which looked like a Rorschach blot. He felt like crying himself.

A lab test would confirm or deny Gray's suspicion, not that it mattered. The truth was he could sympathise with the lonely and tired Nick who'd decided the injustices of the world were too much to bear.

Gray fully understood the pain but was certain no light at the end of the tunnel and no afterlife of angels and virgins existed. Who could believe that?

He asked himself the question for the millionth time – why hadn't *he* ended it all? His subconscious immediately shunted the same old response to the front of his brain.

Unanswered questions.

Ultimately, he couldn't understand why he or anyone else would just give in, even though people made the choice every day. People he'd known. And now this Nick among their unfathomable number.

And what would happen when he had his answers? No idea. Maybe he'd take a dive too. Or step in front of a bus, or maybe drink himself into oblivion. But that was something to consider only when there was clarity, not before.

"You should see the bedrooms," said Fowler.

Fowler led Gray back along the corridor. He pointed to a door on the right and Gray poked his head around the jamb. It was dim in the room, thin curtains firmly closed. An air of decay hung here too.

"Have SOCO been through here?" said Gray. When Fowler nodded, Gray stretched out a hand and flicked on the overhead light. The bulb was one of those weak power savers that took forever to illuminate, and over the course of several minutes brightened to the output of your average pound shop candle.

Gray spent ten seconds examining the interior twice, once more than was required. The room was at best functional, at worst deprived. A plain, rectangular profile, badly painted magnolia walls bereft of decoration, not even any marks from

artworks that may have once hung there. A double bed dominated the room and a low chest of drawers filled the narrow gap
between mattress and wall.

"Not my idea of home."

Gray maintained a tactical silence, reflecting that his own
accommodation was almost as spartan. Instead he turned his
attention to the drawers, slid open the first then the second. He
found dust and condom packets, a few unwrapped, just the foil
left. Gray looked at Fowler for comment, but Fowler was quiet
for once.

Gray switched to the bed. The duvet was askew, rucked,
grimy. Maybe the occupant had just got up. With finger and
thumb he drew back the cover. The sheet below was old, worn,
and stained. Gray dropped the bedding.

"It's a knocking shop?"

"Maybe, hard to say."

"Perhaps the kid was here losing his virginity? He brought
some mistletoe along as a bit of a joke?"

"You tell me."

"It's possible, given the fingerprints. Where are all the
women, though?"

"Why does it have to be women?"

Gray couldn't be bothered with a discussion on sexism and
equal rights, checked his watch instead.

"Is this your number three?" asked Gray.

"No. You'll need to talk to the boss about that."

"Why?"

"Because she said so. I'm just the junior DS around here."
Fowler bared his teeth in a failed attempt at a self-deprecating
smile. "Ah, speak of the she-devil."

DI Hamson – tall, elegant, and well-defined – chose that moment to enter the living room. Her gaze landed heavily on Gray with an expression that said, "Finally."

A phone rang. Gray's. A bright tone that sounded completely out of place in this decrepit flat. Gray scrabbled in his pocket, pulled out his mobile. Once he'd have felt embarrassed being the centre of attention. Now he was accustomed to being stared at, usually in sympathy, sometimes in magnanimity, often in vexation.

"DS Gray."

"Sol, it's Jeff," said Detective Chief Inspector Carslake.

"Carslake," he mouthed to Hamson in an attempt to stem her apparent anger, holding up a finger to say he'd only be a moment. Hamson threw him an irritated look and crossed her arms.

"Where are you?"

"The Slab." Gray identified the brutalist block by his nickname for the place.

"The jumper. What do you think?"

"Not entirely sure. Possibly suicide. We've found a note."

Carslake sighed. He did that a lot, like life was a regular disappointment. "Nothing certain, though."

Suicides had been faked before and would be again. "I know. That's why Forensics are here."

"Keep an open mind."

"Of course."

"Has the pathologist been?"

"Yes, Clough's having his tête-à-tête with the corpse now."

"Okay, good." Gray knew it wasn't. Carslake wasn't a fan of the doctor. The man was too dour, apparently. And Clough didn't drink, a behaviour Carslake treated with a deep suspicion. "I could do with you back here as soon as you can. There's something I'd like to discuss."

Although Gray was keen to avoid the inevitable ruckus at the cordon, Hamson would be keen to know what Carslake wanted with him. The perils of the organisational structure. He'd need to play it carefully, as usual.

"I'm almost finished here. Half an hour okay? It'll take me that long to walk."

"Perfect. There's no need to rush the execution."

"Execution?"

"Just my little joke." It clearly wasn't. "Talk to Hamson first. Then find me in my office."

Where else?

Gray rang off and stuffed the mobile back into a pocket, doubts crowding his mind. What did Carslake want? And why was Hamson even more tense than usual?

"Morning, Yvonne."

"It's Ma'am," said Hamson, agitated. "How many years have I been your boss?"

"Three. So you should know by now."

Hamson bit back a reply. It wasn't as if this was the first time they'd had this discussion. Gray wasn't big on rank, even though Hamson was. Which made him all the more likely to wind her up about it. Most of the time she took it as a joke. Not today.

"Door-to–door is underway," said Hamson to Fowler who was enjoying the spectacle. "Give the PCs a hand."

"*Hold* their hands, more like," said Fowler, though he did as he was told.

Once Fowler left, Hamson's next question was as certain as death and taxes. "What did Carslake want?"

It aggravated Hamson that her boss spent significantly more time with her subordinate than with her. Although Hamson was senior in rank she was junior in years – Gray and Carslake went way back. Close friends at the beginning, although a distance had steadily grown between the men over the years, starting with Tom's disappearance.

"I've been called back to the station," said Gray. "Carslake told me to speak with you first."

"I should bloody well think so. You've got some explaining to do."

"What about?"

Hamson pulled a bagged mobile from her pocket. An old one, scratched and worn. "Recognise this?"

Fowler's item number three.

Ah, shit.

"It's a Nokia," he said.

"Clever. Anything else?"

"Should there be?" He hoped there wasn't, but knew there would.

"It was found down the back of a chair in the living room. Nothing in the memory, except for two numbers. One of them is a dead end. Probably a burner that's been discarded by now."

"The suspense is killing me, Von. Who's the other number?"

Hamson pressed a button on the kid's mobile. Almost immediately Gray's phone began to ring in his pocket.

"Yours."

Three

Hamson showed him the mobile. She was correct. It really was his number in backlit green, identified above with the legend *HELP*.

"I don't understand," he lied.

"That makes two of us. So you know nothing about this?"

"I've never seen him before today." That was the truth, at least.

"Well, he knows you."

"Knows *of* me."

Hamson stared at Gray. He hoped he remained outwardly expressionless as his consciousness churned. He needed to get out, to think. Too much was hitting him at once.

"Do you mind if I catch up on all this later? Carslake's waiting for me," said Gray by way of explanation.

"There'll be questions to answer."

"I'm sure."

"As the DCI's decreed it, not much I can do to stop you, is there?"

"Not really."

Hamson jerked a thumb at his escape route. "Go on, then. Piss off."

"Ma'am."

On the way out, Gray peeled off his overalls and overshoes and slapped them into the open palm of Brian Blake, the increasingly overweight and balding Crime Scene Manager who possessed more than a touch of the superiority complex.

"You didn't check in with me," complained Blake. Procedure dictated he keep a list of everyone at the scene. Blake was the go-to guy, a position from which he generated plenty of self-rewarded kudos.

"I'm leaving anyway," said Gray, just to needle him. From the expression on Blake's face, it had the desired effect.

"You leave everything to us, then. As usual."

Gray threw Blake a sloppy approximation of a salute, enjoyed the scowling response and left. Once he'd reclaimed his coat, Gray negotiated his way back to the lift and pressed the down button.

Once the doors closed, Gray spent the brief descent silently screaming, knuckles between his teeth. But by the time the lift bumped to a halt and the doors heaved open he'd managed to compose himself.

Gray stepped into the foyer, then out onto the pavement where it was still cold and crowded with onlookers.

The constable on the cordon nodded as he lifted the tape. Gray manoeuvred past the spectators. He spotted Scully interviewing a willing participant, his digital voice recorder, what used to be called Dictaphones, stuffed under a bulbous nose.

The reporter must have felt eyes on him because he glanced over. The glance became a stare. Scully wiggled his hand by his ear, thumb and little finger extended in an approximation of a phone. Gray responded with a two-finger salute.

Gray had hitched a ride down from the station in a patrol car. He could easily pull one of the constables away to provide a return trip, but he needed the time to himself.

A brisk walk along the seafront, occasionally buffeted by the sharp wind, did little to blow away the cobwebs. The buzz of traffic and the squawk of gulls weighed on him. His spirits were heavy enough at the best of times. The nearing Christmas cheer, the twinkling of lights, and the repetitively chirpy music that flooded out from every doorway he passed did little to help.

Gray wanted to make a phone call. He knew his mobile number had been passed on to the kid, but he couldn't believe Pennance had been so stupid as to allow it to be stored in a phone where it could be found. Where it *was* found. Given his experience, Pennance should have known better.

Gray had two numbers for Pennance: the deactivated burner also listed on Nick's phone and Pennance's work number. Because of who he was and the nature of their relationship, Gray would have to wait until Pennance deigned to get in contact.

Instead he fixated on the great and the good of Margate. Focused on the detail to keep his thoughts from the dead kid.

A young man oblivious to everything but his smart phone.

Two men, similarly bearded, walking their dog together.

An old man riding a bike in shorts and flip flops weaved between the men. Gray noticed he wore a toe ring, of all things.

The smell of vaping smoke. Strawberry mint?

Gray passed the Turner Contemporary art gallery on the last few hundred yards to the station, a steep ascent up Fort Hill after the relative flat. The museum looked like the design was scrawled on the back of a cigarette packet, mostly because it had been. In fact, the scribbled design was temporarily displayed inside, protected by a glass cabinet. As if someone was going to steal it. Gray had seen it on his one and only visit. At least he hadn't paid out of pocket – it was free admission.

Even so, given the choice, Gray would rather step inside the cast concrete construct and gape at inexplicably expensive modern art than speak to Carslake. But orders were orders. He entered the squat, two-storey building by the front door, delivered a quick nod at the apathetic Sergeant Morgan, a man with a large gut and a small moustache, and descended into the depths of the station.

Four

"You can go straight in," said Sylvia in a tone that conveyed both superiority and derision in equal measure. As if she was the one who decided Gray's movements.

Sylvia was Carslake's personal assistant. Her hair and clothes were straight out of the 1950s. When Carslake was there, so was she, whatever the hour, whatever the day.

No fan of Gray's, Sylvia believed he was a drag to Carslake's career prospects. All she wanted for herself and her boss was a cushy job at HQ.

Gray ignored her glare as he strolled past her desk, a strand of gold tinsel stretched across the top of her monitor. He didn't bother to knock on Carslake's closed door.

Carslake was at his desk, writing, the scratch of nib on paper a dead giveaway. The DCI was a traditionalist.

"Take a seat," he said. Carslake had a habit of speaking slowly and carefully, as if he were explaining things to a child or an imbecile. Hamson had often said it was sexist, but Gray didn't take Carslake's behaviour personally.

Gray closed the door and flopped down onto one of the cheap plastic seats facing his boss's desk. The chair creaked in protest as he shifted around, trying to get comfortable.

People never really grew up. Behaviours learnt in the playground and classroom usually carried through to adulthood.

Even the bloody chairs were the same, the teacher's always more comfortable than the pupil's.

The office was as bare as Gray's fridge, giving the impression of only temporary residence. Carslake's desk was empty, apart from an overflowing in-tray, an ink pot, and the folder in front of him.

Tidy desk, tidy mind was one of Carslake's well-worn mottos. A filing cabinet lurked in a corner, flanked by a coat stand where a grey mackintosh dangled from a brass hook, and a bookshelf boasted a pair of official photos and some Christmas cards.

An overhead bulb threw out a thin, reedy light, softened and warmed by a lampshade ~ no doubt positioned by Sylvia. The cheap plastic blinds were open, revealing the same bland aspect of sea and sky that he'd seen from Arlington House, albeit at a shallower angle. Beyond the cards, Gray was glad to see no Christmas decorations had crept into the room. At least one other person round here was being sensible.

Carslake's austere attitude was a way of separating home from work, to ensure one did not intrude too far into the other. Although it was impossible to achieve completely, a long and happy marriage and several children (now at university) attested to the relative success of his approach. Whereas Gray's marriage had long since flushed itself down the toilet. There was no one left except his daughter Hope, and she was living God knows where. Wherever she was, she wasn't interested in her dad.

Carslake let Gray stew for a minute while he wrote. Gray stretched out in the hope that minimising contact with the chair would provide more comfort. It didn't.

"Paperwork, the curse of seniority," said Gray in an attempt to break the silence.

Carslake, as if waking up to Gray's presence, placed his pen carefully on the desk, and ran stubby fingers through sandy, slightly silvering, hair. He appeared fit and healthy, a good colour to his skin despite the winter gloom.

"Sarcasm becomes you, Sol."

"I know. I've worked hard on it."

"Little else, though."

Gray wasn't sure whether Carslake was joking. It felt more like a rebuke. One that was unfair.

"You've got some explaining to do," said Carslake. He stared impassively at Gray, his fingers interlocked and his fore-arms resting on the paperwork he'd been poring over. The DCI's nails were nicely manicured, unlike Gray's.

"I'm lost. What's to explain?"

"A phone, with your number on it. At a crime scene."

Feigning confusion Gray said, "It's as much a surprise to me as it is to everyone else."

Carslake sighed, gave a slight shake of the head. This time, Gray allowed the silence to stretch, and let Carslake be the one to break it.

"What's going on, Sol?"

"I've no idea what you mean."

"Who's the suicide?"

Gray knew Carslake would be aware of all the facts as soon as they came in. He also knew that he was being probed, the DCI looking for chinks in his armour. "All I know is he was called Nick. I don't think he's been properly identified yet."

Not by us, anyway.

"I don't like this. There will be questions from upstairs."

"There always are. But the thing is, Jeff, we work on the principle of innocent until proven guilty. So I'll say it again, I don't know the kid."

Gray had backed Carslake into a corner. It was a case now of either being called a liar or producing some evidence which countered Gray's claim and laid bare his deceit.

"Okay, Sol. I'll take you at your word."

Bad idea.

Gray stood. "I'd better get back to it, then."

"Sit down, I'm not finished with you yet," said Carslake. "Doctor Mallory ring any bells?"

"Not particularly. Who is he?"

"A private clinician retained by Kent Police. You were supposed to see him."

"Was I?"

Carslake answered with a glare. "This is getting tedious, Sol. Cut the crap."

Deciding to fight fire with fire, to draw attention from his bigger transgression, Gray jerked up out of the seat. He leaned over the desk, looming over the startled Carslake. "Why the bloody hell should I?"

These days they were equal only in age. Rank was something he no longer aspired to and there was a tension between the men.

"Because I'm telling you so, DS Gray. It's how it works. I'm the boss, remember?"

How could he forget? Gray flopped back down in the chair.

"Sylvia said you deliberately avoided her whenever she tried to pin you down about the appointments."

Bloody Sylvia, wreaking her petty revenge. "I've been busy, sir." Gray could get all formal too.

"Really?" Carslake sounded unconvinced.

"Really."

"Well, to avoid any further confusion another appointment has been booked for you."

"My casework–"

"Can be put on hold for an hour. I want to see what Doctor Mallory thinks of you."

"I can say what I'll think of him."

"You've never even met the good doctor. He's new and I anticipate his opinion will be more balanced and professional than yours."

"Ouch, that hurts."

Carslake failed to see the humour. "It was meant to." He moved around the desk and sat on one corner, perched above Gray. Thankfully Carslake refrained from swinging his leg.

"Why are you making me do this?" asked Gray.

"I have to, it's procedure. My hands are tied." Carslake sighed. "Look, Sol, you really need to pay attention to this. If you see a shrink, it means I can keep Professional Standards off both our backs should push come to shove again. Don't you want that?"

"Everyone has bad days."

"With your history you're not even allowed average days."

Gray tensed, saw the regret immediately slide across the DCI's face, a half-formed apology on his lips. An uncomfortable silence fell across the office as the old wound briefly bled, never quite cauterised for either man.

"Once. I lost it once."

"And the reason was understandable." Carslake clicked his fingers a couple of times. "What was the reporter's name?"

"Scully."

"That's it. There was plenty of sympathy for you. What he wrote was atrocious. But it can't happen again. Times are different, emotions aren't as raw, sympathy isn't as forthcoming. I won't be able to stick my neck out for you again."

Gray remembered the disciplinary hearing and Carslake's defence of him. He reasoned that Sylvia was right to see Gray as a risk. And Carslake was right to make him see a shrink. Carslake ran a hand through his hair once more.

"What I mean is, once your card is marked you have to be whiter than white. Which means occasional visits to the medical experts, okay?"

"What's brought all this on?"

Carslake sighed. "There's no easy way to put it. We - no, *I* - have cut you a lot of slack over the years." Carslake held a hand up when Gray opened his mouth to argue. "Just let me speak. We're all sensitive to your past."

"You can say it, you know," bit back Gray. "Tom, Kate."

"Quite. You've never been the easiest of people to get on with at the best of times and we all know when to steer clear, but there are limits."

"Limits?"

"I'm getting feedback that your behaviour is more erratic than whatever is deemed normal for you."

"Says who?"

"That's immaterial."

"*Who?*"

"More than one person. And no matter how much you press me, I'm not revealing their identities."

"Bastards."

"Nobody's sticking the knife in, Sol. Look, why don't you take some leave? Christmas is coming and you've got plenty of time accrued. Hamson can handle the suicide. Get out of the station, get out of Thanet and go somewhere quiet until you've worked through whatever it is that's on your mind."

The suggestion struck Gray between the eyes like a well-aimed arrow. There wasn't anywhere he fancied going on holiday which meant he'd be stuck in the house alone. He couldn't think of anything worse.

"It's pointless, I'll never be past it."

"Nobody expects you to be." Carslake shifted off the desk. Sagged into his chair. He leaned forward, his fingers steepled, and regarded Gray. He let the silence stretch.

"Nearly a decade," said Carslake eventually. "Unbelievable how time slips by."

"Not for me. Every day since then has felt like an eternity."

"Understandable." Carslake seemed a little embarrassed. Gray didn't feel sorry for him. He should know better. "We've still got the here and now to deal with, and that means the doctor."

"Mallory's a quack! I'll bet a week's wages he has no idea what it's like to be a cop, no matter how many diplomas he has on his walls."

"Apparently he has a background in this sort of stuff."

"Stuff?"

"Stress."

"For God's sake, Jeff."

Carslake sighed. "See Mallory, do what he says. Understood?"

"Not really."

"You're making it increasingly hard for me to look out for you."

Gray didn't trust his mouth and kept it closed.

"I assume by your silence you've taken the point?"

Carslake wouldn't be taking no for an answer so Gray eventually managed a grudging agreement. Not that he had any real choice.

A reassured smile appeared briefly on Carslake's lips. "Well, I'm glad we had this little chat." He sat upright in his seat. "Now bugger off and see Sylvia on your way out."

Gray did as he was told, closed the door silently behind him. Sylvia was holding a slip of paper in her left hand. Gray snatched it out of her fingers as he passed.

"You're welcome," she said. Gray grunted. The sound of Sylvia's fingers tapping at the keyboard followed Gray like nails scraping a blackboard.

Halfway down the stairs Gray felt a vibration on his leg, and he heard the muffled but still irritating ditty. He dug around in a pocket for his mobile. The number was listed as unknown. Against his better judgement Gray answered and a familiar, unpleasant voice wormed its way into his ear.

"Good afternoon, Detective Inspector." It was Ed bloody Scully.

"Sergeant."

"Of course, stupid of me. I was getting ahead of myself. Unlike you."

Gray ignored the insult and the reporter's accompanying chuckle. "What do you want?"

"A quote."

"Seriously?"

"No, don't be ridiculous. I know you'd tell me to shove it."

"That's the first time I've heard you speak sense for a long time."

The reporter laughed. "Don't go repeating that, you'll ruin my reputation."

"My heart bleeds."

"Now who's lying?"

"Look, I'm busy. Spit it out or bugger off."

"With pleasure. Have you got a name for the suicide yet?"

"No comment."

"He looked so young. Such a pity."

Gray knew he'd be a fool to ask, but he couldn't resist. "What is?"

"That there was another kid you couldn't protect."

He gripped the mobile until his knuckles turned white. If the reporter had been within reach Gray would have ripped his head off. "The next time I see you..."

Scully was already gone, his laughter hanging in the air.

Five

Gray held his breath, and his temper, until he hit the car park. He shoved the access door hard. It slammed into the wall, the handle gouging a chunk out of the brickwork. The impact and accompanying bellowed expletive from Gray drew stares from a couple of hardy PCs sucking on cigarettes.

"What?" he spat.

"Nothing, sir," replied the braver of the two women.

"Don't you have work to be getting on with?"

"Yes, sir."

Gray nodded as if to say *get on with it then*, walked the few paces to his car and slid inside. As he put the key into the ignition he checked his rear view. The women were stubbornly sucking down the last of the tar-laden smoke. They skimmed glances in his general direction, drawing the line at a direct stare, muttering between themselves. There was even the brief shake of a head.

Being talked about behind your back again, Sol.

Gray almost got out but stopped himself. They'd done nothing wrong. It was him.

He waited until they ditched the filters and returned to the station before he started the engine of his blocky Saab. It was a bit of a clunker, but always started and was cheap to run. Material objects no longer mattered to Gray. After a brief pause for traffic he swung out onto the road and began the drive home, which, on a good run, would take no more than a quarter of an hour, though there was no such thing as a straightforward route around here.

Just beyond the sprawling hospital grounds, where rough-and-ready Margate became genteel Broadstairs, a sudden impulse struck him.

Instead of going straight over at the Dane Court Road roundabout he turned left into the sleepy parish of St Peters. Not so long ago the village had teemed with life. But once the post office closed, most of the other businesses had slipped away too, one by one. It was like watching a once fit and proud person slide into decay and dementia.

It was the same story all over Thanet, the area which encompassed the three interlinked towns of Margate, Broadstairs, and Ramsgate on the eastern tip of Kent.

He swept by three- and four-storey houses (where the artist William Sickert, a Jack the Ripper suspect, had once resided), a rather good Chinese restaurant, a passable chip shop, and The Red Lion pub before taking another left and pulling in at the rear of a supermarket, about the only business generating any serious revenue round here.

He slammed the door shut and locked up using the key, as the battery in the fob was long dead. For a moment he leaned back against the car and stared at the flint–built church which brooded over the immediate surroundings. A crenelated tower, more like a castle than a place of worship, pushed up towards the heavens and looked over the vicarage and burial ground.

He progressed along a narrow tarmac path, as straight as any Roman road, away from the church, through the markers of the long dead.

He passed a war grave, kept scrupulously clean; then, a few yards further along, a looming angel minus its left arm; and beyond that a formal mausoleum, ringed by a rusty metal fence.

A police officer who'd been killed in the line of duty (shot), his fiancée following on not far behind (cause of death unstated), and a maritime disaster (only the wealthy honoured).

When he passed the tiny stones, the ones for children and babies, Gray looked elsewhere. It was too painful to see the lives of the young cut ludicrously short.

The cemetery had changed since his last visit; a slash and burn policy stripping away the shrubs that had sprung up between the corpses.

It was a shame. Gray had liked the place's unruly appearance, a little life among the dead. A number of the subsequently revealed plots had been reclaimed by the greenery, roots bursting through marble and stone, ivy scarring the dedications. At least they'd had attention from something; touched by the organic. Now the dead were bare and forgotten again. Not even wilted flowers adorned the memorials.

A voice in Gray's head told him to stop. He was at the stone. His eyes skimmed over the first few words. Katherine Gray. *Kate*. She'd passed on five years ago, but she'd been dead inside long before. As Carslake had said, it was incredible how quickly time passed. And yet how slowly.

There was a gravestone to the right of Kate's. Not for him, but for their son, Tom. She'd bought both plots, two graves, without Gray's knowledge, after they were separated. By then she controlled her own finances. The joint account split down the middle, like everything else after their marriage, came to a shuddering halt. No divorce though, because she believed in

the sanctity of the union, and so his surname graced the dedica-
tion. Now everything she once owned was his. Including these
spaces in the earth.

It had been a critical argument between them – whether
Tom was alive or dead. Gray wouldn't give up until he saw
proof; Kate said she knew he was gone. Gray asked how that
was possible; Kate simply pointed to her chest and said it came
from within. From God in her heart.

And where was that higher being when Kate chose to
check out and move on?

That day, Gray had received a panicked phone call from her
best friend, Alice. There was no note. He'd never know what
finally drove Kate to end it all. But he understood what had
started her inevitable slide.

Loss.

Gray couldn't allow his eyes to reach the final letters of the
inscription. He'd never done so in all the days and months after burying her. He turned, retraced his steps faster than the
trudge that had brought him here, his heart pounding.

Gray sank onto a bench, facing a small square of land where
the cremations were consecrated, a rectangular brass plaque for
each life affixed to the floor or wall with undersized screws.
Gray felt his heart gradually slow, his breathing ease from the
fast, short bursts which had previously punctuated his lungs.

Coming here was a mistake.

He felt a spot of rain and groaned at the sight of a black
cloud spreading across the sky, hanging overhead like a shroud.
It seemed to have materialised from nowhere. Another spot of
cold water hit his face, followed a second later by a deluge of

big, fat drops. If he didn't move fast, he'd be soaked. His car was close, but the church was closer.

He made a dash for the church, arm over his head in a vain attempt to keep his hair dry. Soon he was in cover under the arched porch. The rain lashed down now, and it felt like some unseen hand was once more directing Gray's actions.

He grabbed the heavy iron handle set into the studded wooden door and twisted. With some effort, he hefted the ancient latch. The door, designed in architectural sympathy with the porch, swung back on massive, well-oiled hinges. He stepped inside and pushed it closed again. The fall of the bar echoed around the cool, dim space.

Gray negotiated a couple of sandstone steps, each worn into a smile by many feet over many years, sinners and penitents alike. Few of either visited these days, however. The interior was of the standard layout. Nave, chancel, altar, and parallel rows of pews, each of them sporting half-finished seasonal wreaths. The periphery, though, was beyond the standard. A magnificent vault and impressive stained glass windows behind the pulpit separated St Peter's Church from the mundane rest.

Blessed are the poor.

It was ironic. If the priesthood had built simple structures and distributed the excess donations between its parishioners, then perhaps today there would be a more even spread of wealth and happiness in current society. The religious order had fallen foul of one of its own sins.

It was an unpopular view Gray had ceased to voice long before terminating his attendance at Sunday services. Here was another rift between husband and wife following Tom's disappearance – as Gray drifted away from religion, so Kate became more committed to the Lord's word.

He wandered the perimeter, glancing at metal and stone plaques affixed to the wall, praising the virtuous and pious. It didn't take long; this was a diminutive church in a pocket-sized village. Once it was different. Saint Augustine had landed just up the coast at Minster a millennium ago, returning Christianity to Britain. The first cathedral founded in nearby Canterbury. Senior religious figures regularly made the trip to the continent and vice versa. That was a glory long, long past.

The leaded windows were set too high in the wall for Gray to see much, just a patch of ponderous sky and streams of water cascading down the glass. The rain tap danced on the roof.

He took a pew. The varnished wood was uncomfortable, and it wasn't long before he felt a chill through the seat of his trousers. He leaned forward slightly for comfort, arms on his thighs, then sat back again when he realised he was in a prayer position.

Many significant events in his life had happened right here. A marriage, a baptism, a funeral, every one of them attended by Jeff Carslake, even though in the end it had felt as if Carslake was fulfilling an obligation.

The rattle of the latch pierced his thoughts. Someone was backing in, shaking out an umbrella into the porch so the water wouldn't dot the brown tiles underfoot.

The person turned around, unsurprised to find someone else here. Their eyes met. Gray took in the middle-aged man: soft face, round glasses, thinning hair. Dressed entirely in black, except for the dog collar about his neck, so white it should be in a washing powder advert.

"David. Just my luck," Gray murmured.

Reverend David Hill propped his damp umbrella against the wall. "It's my church. You should have known I would likely be here."

"The thought hadn't crossed my mind," said Gray. He wasn't telling the entire truth. "And isn't it God's house?"

The vicar smiled and pointed at the pew Gray was occupying. "May I?"

"It's your church. You can sit where you like."

"I wouldn't want to intrude."

"That's what you lot do though, isn't it? Meddle whether people want it or not?"

"Perhaps sometimes *people*, as you put it, don't know they're in need of an intervention until it happens."

"I didn't come looking for you or a saviour, David. I was just getting out of the rain."

"Bit out of your way though, isn't it?"

Gray ignored the question. A silence fell, punctuated by the staccato patter of the downpour. He kept his gaze forward, studying the detail in the stained-glass windows. Christ being crucified right in the centre.

"How are you keeping?" asked David.

"So that took, what?" Gray made a show of checking his watch. "Thirty seconds? You'd make a dreadful criminal. Children can stay quiet for longer than that."

"I was just being polite."

"Right." Another pause. "You're going to keep asking me, aren't you?"

"Yes."

Gray noted the self-assurance in the other man's voice. He held his temper. For Kate. Because her belief had strengthened, even as Gray's resolve had collapsed to dust. Because despite it all, Gray still loved her. Always would.

David was talking again. "We'd welcome you back with open arms. Come and join us again. Please, Sol."

"You make it sound like a cult."

"For some, maybe it is, although one of love and support. And you haven't answered my question. How are you?"

"I'm fine."

"Then why are you here?"

"I told you."

"To get out of the rain," David repeated. "Except I don't believe that."

"Did God whisper otherwise into your ear?" scoffed Gray.

"I saw you from the vicarage window. You were in the graveyard."

Gray flinched, like a secret had been physically yanked out of him. He clamped his jaw tight, not trusting his mouth right now.

"Did you go and see her?" David didn't say Kate's name and Gray was oddly grateful for it.

Gray nodded. "I don't know why, before you ask."

"The why doesn't matter, Sol. It's important that you did."

Gray could feel the anger boiling up in him. The vicar's words now sounded more sanctimonious than sympathetic.

"Five years since she died. That's long enough, isn't it?"

"You mean killed herself, Reverend. A sinful act."

David stared down at his feet, uncomfortable with Gray's statement.

Tough. It was the truth and the truth always had to be revealed, whatever the implications.

"Do you know what I witnessed today?" asked Gray, twisting the knife. "Another wasted life. Another idiot who thought the best option was to check out. He was a teenager. Seventeen, eighteen at the most. Threw himself off Arlington House."

"I'm sorry you had to see that, Sol."

"Why? Why does the All-Powerful who resides in the Heavens allow this to happen? And don't say it's a test."

"How old would Tom be now?"

"Don't talk in the past tense about him. He's still alive, I know it." His voice was low and full of conviction.

"Sorry. It wasn't intentional. But it's been ten years, Sol. Maybe it's time to move on?"

"Like Kate did, you mean?"

The vicar shook his head. "I didn't come here for an argument. In fact, I wanted your help with something."

"Not matters of the church, I hope?"

"Just the opposite. The work of the devil, actually."

"What?"

"It's a fight with evil. One you're uniquely qualified to aid me with."

Gray was about to respond when the scrape of wood on stone signified the church door was opening once more. A woman this time. She wore a coat and one of those clear, plastic hoods to keep the rain off. Through it, Gray could see white hair.

Alice Newbold, a parishioner, the most dedicated of them all and Kate's best friend at the end. It was Alice and Margaret Fowler - Mike Fowler's wife - who kept the church running.

They were firm advocates of David Hill. Alice had been coming to the church forever, more so once her husband, a veteran of the Second World War and subsequent pillar of the community, had passed on, leaving little else of substance in her life.

Alice stopped in her tracks, taking in Gray's presence with the vicar, clearly unsure how to deal with this unexpected vision. Eventually she broke the silence. "I'm only here to finish off the decorations."

Gray stood. "I'll take *that* as a sign from above." He decided to take the long way out, along the nave, rather than cramming past David. He paused at the reverend's shoulder, bent over and spoke into his ear: "He's sixteen and he's out there somewhere, I just haven't found him yet. And I won't stop until I do."

Gray gave Alice a nod as he passed. He liked her, although she had a tendency to interfere in the name of the righteous and he wasn't in the mood for it just now.

"You're welcome here any time, Solomon," said Alice.

"Who says I want to be?"

"Kate does."

Gray stepped out into the torrent before he said something he'd regret.

Six

As Gray walked the final few yards to his car, the deluge eased to a fine drizzle. Margaret Fowler passed him on the way – him leaving, her arriving. She was a slight woman: short, thin, and bird-like with a carefully made-up face. She was so different from her husband. He exchanged the briefest of greetings with her.

The temperature had plummeted with the sinking sun, the angry red orb partially hidden by oppressive clouds. Gray slid inside his car, cringing at the touch of damp clothes against his skin. He started the engine, turned the heaters on full.

During the short drive, Gray reflected on his discussion with Hill, wondering what he meant about the devil's work, dismissing it as another lure, and a stupid one at that. If he wasn't careful, Hill and Alice would be sucking him back in again. Gray would ask Carslake to shoot him first.

He found a spot on a street not far from home, locked up and hustled himself into a walk. Christmas trees shimmered in every window he passed. Most houses sported lights hanging from the roof. His didn't. Gray was the Grinch of his neighbourhood.

This had once been the Gray family home. Now it was simply a place to exist, a terraced house keeping the weather off a handful of immaterial objects. It had the original wooden windows where everyone else's were plastic, a slate roof with a few slipped tiles and a narrow, bare front garden. Gray didn't possess green fingers.

The majority of the neighbours were families or had been once; it was that sort of area. Good schools nearby, the houses a decent enough size to make the two-point-four children feel like not such a constriction of adult life. God knows, you gave up enough to become a parent.

Gray caught himself. *There I go again. Calling on the bloody Almighty.*

Why? It wasn't like Gray believed in a higher being any more. How could he? Each to their own, though where was the evidence? God had forsaken the Grays. He'd worked hard to repay the favour and would go on doing so until all was square.

When they'd first acquired the house their expenses stretched to bursting point, especially once Kate, a copper herself, gave up work to focus on the pregnancy. He'd told her it was too big a financial burden. She'd held firm. She wanted somewhere they could call their own, and what husband could truly disagree with his wife in that respect? And ultimately it was for their unborn child, a girl, Hope. And a few years later one became two, a boy, Thomas.

Gray worked extra hours to earn more money, decorated the house in whatever little spare time he had, did everything to make it right. And it worked. For a while they'd been blissfully happy, a promotion to sergeant alleviating the financial anxiety.

With Tom's disappearance, the life they'd built came crashing down. Kate blamed Gray. He moved out and rented a flat, which only darkened the house's innards further when Kate died. This was a residence of grim memory, of what might have been, but never would be.

Gray slid the key into the lock and twisted. It was the same set he'd always owned. When the house became his again, Kate's stuff ended up in the loft or dumped in the charity shop. He flicked on the hallway light. The furnishings were as bland as Carslake's office. These days, belongings weren't replaced until broken or worn out beyond repair. That was the one decent lesson his father had taught him.

Gray scooped the post from the floor. A mix of bills, junk mail, and season's greetings. All three would end up in the bin. He tramped along the hallway, past the ornate banister, down a couple of steps into the narrow kitchen which overlooked a hideously tangled garden, all leggy grass, mighty stinging nettles and tortuous brambles.

Gray part-filled the kettle and set it on the stove. He got the coffee out of the fridge and scooped grounds into a French press. It didn't matter whether he drank caffeine late at night or not. How much sleep he didn't enjoy was determined by his subconscious mind alone.

While the kettle juddered, he thought back to an article he'd read a few days ago that claimed people who believed in higher beings tended to live longer than those who did not. Gray didn't have a problem with the statistic in particular, beyond the fact he'd no desire to spend any longer on earth than was absolutely necessary.

No, it was the basis for the conclusion, that religious types bore less of a burden, believing the Almighty would take care of everything. Despite so much evidence to the contrary.

Gray knew they were fools. In the absence of an all-powerful existence in the heavens it was left to people like him, the police, to protect others. Although when it had come to his own family, he'd utterly failed.

He trotted up the three sets of stairs to the loft room where he slept and searched his many files until he found what he wanted. Stories neatly snipped from newspapers, held together by a paper clip.

By the time Gray got back to the kitchen, steam was billowing from the kettle's spout. He flicked off the gas, sloshed hot water onto the grounds. From a bottom drawer he retrieved a scotch bottle, blend not malt, and poured a slug into a mug.

While he waited for the coffee to brew, he flicked through the handful of articles. All were written by the leech, Scully, charting Gray's disasters. Tom, Kate, the assault and subsequent suspension from the force. Not his reappointment, of course. Scandal sells, good news doesn't.

The earliest article featured a photo of Gray, an expression that portrayed his loss and desolation. Then a second, more studied, image of the stuff he'd won at the fair for Tom. A teddy bear and a goldfish, discarded and trampled into the muddy ground. The former grubby, the latter dead.

Gray stared at the picture of his younger self, on the cusp of seeing the world as a far darker place than even he had realised.

Seven

Ten Years Ago

He loved tucking Tom up in bed so he was warm and comfortable. That's what fathers were for. A broad smile split Tom's face, happy they were together. Gray grinned back, a contented man. He ruffled Tom's short, dark hair. He had his mother's looks: big blue eyes and high cheekbones. Short for his age. He also had Kate's temperament, rarely speaking but certain of his views when he did.

The lamp beside Tom's bed spilled out a pocket-sized pool of light against the darkness of night. The animals on Tom's wallpaper were dim shades of themselves, a mobile hung above his bed. His choice, Gray's hard work to put up. He hadn't minded at all.

"What story do you want?" asked Gray, already knowing the answer. He held the book clasped between his knees. Tom was sure to have seen it.

"Gingerbread man!" he shouted. Voice full of glee. Innocent. For now. Until tomorrow.

"What, again?"

"Yes, please. Again!"

"Don't you want something else? You've got so many books."

Tom owned a shelf unit full. Fables and fiction, tall tales and short stories. Gray pointed, went to pull one down, kept the other behind his back.

"Gingerbread man," said Tom firmly, shaking his head.

"All right then," said Gray. He sat back down on the bed. Tired springs creaked.

Gray lifted the book. Tilted it toward the light, so Tom could stare at the familiar pictures. They knew all the words, although Tom could only read very slowly.

"Once upon a time," started Gray, "there was a little old man and a little old woman..."

Tom's eyes were as wide as an owl's.

"... the little gingerbread man ran away as fast as his little legs would carry him..."

"Run, run as fast as you can, you can't catch me, I'm the gingerbread man," they both rhymed.

Gray laughed when the gingerbread man escaped the old couple and the cow. Tom pulled the covers up to his nose when the gingerbread man met the fox, buried his head completely once the fox threw the gingerbread man up in the air and *snap!* Gray always slapped the book shut at this point. Sharp teeth on soft flesh. The fox made Tom quail. Gray told him he was safe.

"Get some sleep now, son," said Gray, bending down and kissing his forehead. "Tomorrow's your big day."

"I promise I won't be able to sleep, Daddy."

"Then you'll miss your birthday and not go to the fun fair. Do you want that?"

Tom shook his head.

"I didn't think so."

Gray flicked off the bedside lamp, plunging the room into darkness. Tom uttered a little whimper.

"Can you leave the door open, Daddy?" asked Tom. Gray did so, a strip of light from the bulb on the landing falling across Tom's bed.

"Thanks, Daddy."

"Night, son."

Gray withdrew from the room, watched through the crack as Tom snuggled down beneath the pile of blankets that pressed around him like a comforting arm. Gray caught another smile when Tom's feet touched the hot water bottle he'd snuck in while his son was brushing his teeth.

Tomorrow he'd be six. This was the last time Tom would sleep in his own bed. Maybe the last time he'd feel loved without having to relinquish something of himself.

Gray should have known, because that's what fathers were for, but he didn't.

"Sleep tight," whispered Gray.

As for Gray, he would never sleep tight again.

Eight

During the blackest hours the angst crept in, disturbing his hard-won slumber. Gray's eyes snapped open. The voice of the dead kid, Nick, speaking to him from beyond the grave, still fresh in his mind.

Gray exhaled, staring into darkness. He couldn't see what time it was. He hated digital clocks with their bright displays, and relied instead on his digital watch. He pressed a button next to the dial which dimly lit the screen. It said 5:00 a.m.

His sleep pattern varied from day to day. Sometimes he'd wake in the middle of the night. Other times he'd sleep right through to morning. In either case, he never felt refreshed. His mind wouldn't allow him a proper respite.

Gray occupied a double bed at the very top of the building. It was the most indifferent of spaces, though that didn't matter. Here he was furthest away from the families around him and the rooms where his family had slept. The greatest distance away from the greatest catastrophe in his life.

It was a bizarre thing, anxiety. In the brightness of a new day it retreated to the dark corners of his mind. As the afternoon wore on it would stick out a tentative toe, and in the wee hours it leapt forward like the tide, filling the pools of his subconscious with stagnant memories.

The early days after he lost Tom were a harrowing period. Gray found it nearly impossible to cope. His world narrowed to the moment he was in, everything else was miserable shadow.

Five years of keeping it together, and then Kate... After that, he could take no more.

Carslake had found Gray in the empty bath, surrounded by a scattering of pills. Gray was fully clothed, a bottle of vodka in his hand.

Gray hadn't attempted to kill himself, despite appearances to the contrary. It was just that at times everything would go dark, like a veil passed over his eyes, and he just wanted to sleep. Without dreaming.

Carslake got Gray help and for a few weeks the meds prescribed by Doctor Stone actually made Gray feel worse, increasing his depression. He'd finally settled and felt calmer. For a while. But once he realised the drugs had become a crutch, he stopped taking them and gave up seeing the doctor.

As a result, Gray had no desire to see this Doctor Mallory, Stone's successor, despite Carslake's insistence. Mallory would just prescribe more chemicals. Gray still kept some in the drawer next to his bed. Like a smoker with a permanently unopened pack of cigarettes. In case of emergency...

He'd have to deal with it at some point.

But for now, Gray had to get up. He sat upright, causing paper to cascade off his chest and onto the floor.

"Ah, shit!"

Gray remembered now that he'd taken his coffee and retreated to bed, tucking duvets and covers around him, pillows at his back. It was a ritual. Every evening he went over Tom's case hoping he'd missed some clue. That he'd fallen asleep partway through was unusual. Waking up without remembering, even more so. It wasn't a good sign.

Gray fumbled for the lamp switch and flicked it on. He carefully peeled back the bed covers so not to disturb the other documentation. Papers dotted the floor space in neat little piles. Elsewhere, there were folders, newspaper clippings, and printouts from articles he'd found on the web, all catalogued in files stacked next to each other on shelves. All precisely catalogued, dated, and ordered.

Gray knew the location of every individual record. Most were duplicates of police archives, stuff he'd copied and smuggled out under the noses of his colleagues. Stuff he shouldn't have. Just possessing copies was gross misconduct, maybe even grounds for dismissal. But how else was he to carry on the investigation into Tom's disappearance?

He slipped out of bed, shivered in the chilly air, then bent down to gather up the tumbled sheets. He kept a small fan heater nearby and switched it on now, the venting angled so the air blew upwards and didn't disturb the papers. He refused to switch on the central heating. What was the point in thawing out such a large house when all he occupied was the one room?

He hastened to gather the last few sheets, not willing to wait for sunlight in case something ended up mislaid and out of order. That single piece of paper might have the key. He still believed this, despite having read every last page of every last document in the room at least a hundred times over the last decade. Most of the articles he could recite from memory, just like *The Gingerbread Man*. Nothing had been missed; it wasn't there to be found. But Gray couldn't admit that to himself.

The book was on his bedside cabinet. *The Gingerbread Man.* Gray grabbed hold of it and, with a shiver, clambered gratefully back under the covers. He turned off the lamp before wrapping the blankets like a cocoon around him. He listened to the hum of the heater as he fingered the book's worn spine.

The upset and fear would sit in his stomach all night now, gnawing away like a rat on gristle. Gray lay foetus-like, arms crossed over his chest, the memory gripped between his fingers. Unblinking eyes stared into the darkness, reliving that night.

Yet again.

Nine

Holding a steaming coffee cup, Gray surveyed his garden. He pondered whether today was the day to finally get on with clearing the weeds, but hoped it would rain again so he couldn't. Then again, beyond decimating the mini-jungle, Gray had no idea what to do with himself. Leisure time was a rare and difficult-to-manage event. He gave silent thanks when his mobile rang. It was nearby just in case Pennance decided to call.

He hadn't, of course. The bastard had left him twisting in the wind.

"Saved by the bell," he said. He checked the display, saw it was Hamson, and decided to answer even though it was his day off. "Morning, Von."

"It's Ma'am."

"I know."

Hamson sighed. "Any plans for the day?"

"The lawn needs napalming. Why, have you got something for me?"

"Just being polite before we get into the grit."

"Sounds ominous."

"More than having your number on a dead kid's phone?"

"I've been over that. With you and Carslake."

"Yes, he told me. He also told me Blake's been complaining about you."

The Crime Scene Manager, causing trouble again. Hamson and Blake had a well-known dislike of each other following a particularly uncomfortable Christmas party. Blake had left his wife, and, in front of the whole office, declared undying love for Hamson. She laughed in his face.

"What was Blake complaining about this time? Global warming? The state of the economy? Immigration, perhaps?"

"His displeasure at your all-too-brief appearance at Nick Buckingham's flat."

"Ah, we have the lad's name."

"You're choosing to ignore the Crime Scene Manager's criticism?"

"I was under orders to return to the station. What's your second point?"

"I've already said."

"All I've heard so far is bleating from Blake."

"Nicholas Buckingham. Fingerprints came through on the victim."

"Strictly, Von, he wasn't a victim. He died by his own hand."

"Also, he was sixteen, Sol. A child."

Hamson's utterance stabbed Gray through the heart. Sixteen. Same age as Tom. He looked older. Or maybe Gray just wanted him to be older, so he couldn't be Tom.

Gray ended the call, even though Hamson was still talking. He held the phone loosely in his hand, staring into the distance.

No way he'd get to the garden today.

AN HOUR LATER, SHAVED and showered, Gray was at the Margate station, his rare weekend off discarded. He found DS Fowler in the incident room, writing up details about Nick Buckingham onto a whiteboard. At the top was the deceased's name, then underneath was the information they'd gathered so far and several colour photographs of the cadaver in situ. It wasn't much to go on.

"So you got the short straw," said Gray.

"Bloody hell, you scared the crap out of me!" Fowler's neck and cheeks turned red with anger and embarrassment. Gray ignored Fowler's discomfort; he'd get over it, and Gray was keen to voice the question at the forefront of his mind.

"I understand the jumper has been identified?"

"We found a match in no time. He had priors."

"Why didn't anyone tell me? I had to hear about it from Hamson."

"I left a message on your voicemail."

"You did?"

"That's what normal people do when the other party doesn't answer their phone."

Gray took a moment to check. There was indeed a text telling him a message awaited his attention.

"Next time, try harder."

"It's your weekend off."

"I don't care whether I'm at work or not."

"Your call."

"I'll live. Give me a quick run down."

"Not much to say, really. Sixteen years old, from London originally, a load of arrests up there until a few months back when he dropped off the radar."

"Any pulls here?"

"Nothing official."

"So he ended his life of crime, then?"

Gray saw the beginnings of a restrained shrug.

"Couldn't say."

"What about benefits?" It was common for people on the dole to relocate down to the coast to sign on. The money was the same, but the air quality and the view were a drastic improvement over inner city squalor. The flat and Buckingham's living expenses would be covered by the taxpayer, of course.

"Nothing. Unless he was operating under a different name."

"Take his photo down to the benefits office when they reopen on Monday and see if anyone recognises him."

"Who put you in charge?"

"Hamson, remember? Anything from the door-to-door?"

"Nothing meaningful."

"What a surprise."

"A couple of the flats didn't answer, including the immediate neighbours. Otherwise nobody saw or heard anything."

"Get a uniform back to the ones who weren't interviewed and make sure they are this time."

"Sure."

"And find out who owns the flat."

Gray left Fowler to his scribbling and headed to his desk. Once he'd flopped into the ancient chair, he dragged his keyboard over and accessed the Missing Persons logs, both regional and national. Nobody named Nicholas Buckingham had been reported missing within the last five years.

Perhaps he had parents who weren't interested in his welfare? A more charitable assumption would be the lad was an orphan. Although if he'd been in care, why hadn't the supporting organisation flagged up his disappearance? Perhaps they had, and it had been recorded as an absence, a lower-tier description of missing that didn't warrant police time. Sometimes kids slipped through the net as a result.

He switched over to the Police National Computer, tapped in the deceased's name. This time there was a hit - many, in fact. A long list of misdemeanours from shoplifting upwards. The last notation was an arrest in London six months ago, the charge: vagrancy and disorderly conduct. Nick had been lifted in Green Park, one of the most affluent areas of the city, given a caution, and referred to his social worker. The reason why wasn't detailed. Gray wrote down the name of the arresting officer, a PC Yandell, followed by the social worker, Rosemary Dent.

Another couple of clicks and Buckingham's mugshot popped up on the screen. The eyes were bright and strong, glaring out of a face loaded with anger. Gray felt another, stronger tug of guilt. Why hadn't he paid more attention yesterday?

Gray sent the information on Buckingham to the printer and launched another programme, SLEUTH, which revealed significantly more detail and made for grim reading. Buckingham had barely been at the series of schools he was supposed to attend. He'd moved around a lot, a foster kid. He was a troublemaker and was difficult to manage. Presumably they were just glad to see the back of him, hence the lacking notation on MisPers. No wonder the poor sod had ended it all. He wasn't exactly leaving much behind.

With a little effort, Gray found the numbers for both Yandell and Dent. He picked up the phone and dialled. He got lucky.

"Hello, PC Yandell speaking."

The accent was Home Counties. Gray introduced himself. The PC didn't warm up at the sound of a fellow copper. Just the opposite, in fact.

"What's this about?" asked Yandell.

"An arrest you made earlier in the year. Nick Buckingham."

"You'll have to give me more than that," said Yandell, sounding exasperated, like Gray was some sort of idiot.

Gray summarised Yandell's arrest report to a few moments of silence.

"I vaguely remember him, sir. I think me and my partner arrested him. Then again, I might be wrong. I'd have to get my notebook to be certain."

"So, unremarkable then."

Yandell seemed distinctly disinterested. "His sort are ten-a-penny here, sir."

"Sad."

"It's the world we live in. Look, I've got to shift it. Briefing's in a few minutes. I need a cuppa first, know what I mean?"

"Not really," said Gray.

But Yandell was gone.

Gray tried Dent next. The response was voicemail, a message that she was unavailable and to leave a message or call another number if it was an emergency. Which it wasn't, so he hung up. Gray drew several circles around Dent's name. He'd try again on Monday.

There was still Marcus Pennance. Gray stayed his hand. He wasn't supposed to know Pennance, and the man operated across blurred lines. It meant he got things done, but Gray didn't always like the methods. He definitely didn't like suicide victims ending up with his number on their mobiles. Detective Inspector Pennance had some explaining to do. But for now he'd have to wait.

Fowler dropped the printed mugshot of Buckingham onto Gray's desk. "Funny. I've been staring at his face for hours and he reminds me of someone."

"Who?"

"You, Sol. He looks like you."

Gray leapt up and grabbed Fowler by the throat, then threw him onto the floor. Fowler hit the ground hard. Gray raised his fist to punch Fowler but he held back.

"Go on then," said Fowler. "Hit me!"

"You're not worth it." Gray stepped back, grabbed his coat from the back of his chair and left the office.

Ten

Up in the gods, the motor kicked into life and cables shifted as the lift made its slow descent to the ground floor. Gray jangled the flat keys in his pocket while he waited. He took a long look at the mugshot of Buckingham.

Is there a resemblance?

Distracted, Gray answered his ringing mobile. "Hello?"

"Good morning, Solomon. It's David Hill. Do you have a minute?"

Gray closed his eyes. The last thing he needed was Reverend Hill on his back. "I'm always here for the devil's work."

There was a pause as Hill digested the sarcasm. It didn't seem to put him off. "I need your help."

"So you said. With what?"

"I've been investigating things myself."

"Things?"

"Yes. It's best I show you. Can you come over here?"

The lift shuddered to a stop in front of him. Gray stepped inside and the doors closed. He pressed number five. The panel was worn and scratched where thousands of fingers had prodded at it over the years. The interior still smelled faintly of urine. He figured it was probably a spray the cleaners used.

"I don't know, David. I'm busy."

"It's very important." Gray could hear the desperation in his tone. "I wouldn't ask otherwise."

The lift began to ascend.

"Maybe. I'm not promising anything."

But David Hill was gone. The signal had dropped out.

The lift jerked to a halt at the third floor. No one was there. On again to five. The doors stuck halfway open and Gray had to turn sideways to escape. The entrances to the flats were firmly barred and stretched off to the left and right.

For a moment Gray wondered if he'd recognise the location. Yesterday it had been obvious, the entrance gaping like a missing tooth. Gray hadn't taken a note of the number, never expecting to return, but the blue-and-white police tape was a giveaway. As was the replacement door. It looked wrong. Renewal among the refuse. Gray's phone rang again, but he ignored it.

He jerked the tape down, slid the key into the lock and twisted. It moved easily. New, well-oiled, not even slightly worn. After pausing a moment to allow his eyes to adjust to the dim corridor, Gray gave the residence another inspection.

The bathroom hadn't been part of his assessment the first time around. He noted a dark ring mark around the scratched bath, mould in the corners of the shower, a split plastic curtain. The toilet seat was down. He didn't fancy peering into its depths but did so anyway, relieved there were no nasty surprises.

The bedrooms were carbon copies of each other, scruffy and cheap, identically furnished and already familiar to Gray. The kitchen was plain, dirty dishes piled in the sink, cupboards almost bare, as was the fridge, which hummed away in the corner. The light didn't come on when he opened the door. A sour odour wafted out. A half pint of milk at the back, probably cottage cheese by now.

Finally, Gray entered the living room at the end of the corridor. A layer of fingerprint dust covered everything. Whoever lived here next would struggle to get rid of the bloody stuff. The few sticks of furniture were out of position on the worn carpet, if the indentations were anything to go by. Shifted by the investigators.

Hamson had said the mobile was found down the back of a seat. There were a couple you'd expect to see around a table, all hard wood and functional. Just one armchair, facing the floor-to-ceiling window. The Slab might be a monstrosity from another era, but it had a hell of a view.

Resolving to wash his hands afterwards, Gray poked his fingers between the cushions and felt around. He pulled out plenty of fluff and hair, but nothing meaningful. Not even cash. Perhaps the phone had slipped out of Buckingham's pocket, ended up wedged in the constricted space.

There was one last location he hadn't checked. He didn't want to now, but he had no choice. He grabbed the handle of the French window, his palm sweaty. His heart accelerated. He didn't like heights, liked sheer drops even less, and the thought of going outside terrified him.

After a deep breath and a steeling of nerves, Gray jerked the window open. Immediately he was buffeted by the wind which tore unhindered straight across the North Sea. He stepped over the threshold and the wind pushed and slapped at him a little more. Bizarrely, even through the turmoil, he could smell fag smoke. Probably another resident having a crafty cigarette.

Gray took a moment to further compose himself, to allow the anxiety to ease as his mind became accustomed to this new state of affairs. Like many with a fear of heights, Gray felt an impulse to throw himself over the edge. He hated the feeling, that sensation of being on the brink of losing control.

Gray shuffled the final few feet to the end of the balcony and peered over the edge, his hands tightly gripping the rusty railing which flaked old paint at his touch. The metal shifted under his grasp and the dread rushed up again, squeezed his heart, constricted his throat. Gray took a rapid step back, leaned against the exterior wall and gulped down air. But, before his brain could argue, he returned to the railing and peered down at the pavement.

He didn't want to imagine what would drive someone to dive into nothing, to watch the solid mass race towards their face, unable to turn back, unable to change their mind. Fearless or fearful, he couldn't decide.

Gray stepped away once more from the edge. His pulse didn't slow until the window was closed and the sound of the wind receded to a whisper. He exhaled through pursed lips, and sucked in another breath to calm himself down.

There was no more to see here. Perhaps Blake's report, once he released it, would provide more clues. Or perhaps it really had been a pointless death.

GRAY WAS REPLACING the tape when he heard a cough, a single, sharp hack. He ignored it, but there was a second cough, followed by a third. He turned to see an obese man leaning in a neighbouring doorway. He was dressed all in black, jet black hair tied back in a ponytail in the style of a goth. Maybe the hint of some eyeliner.

The goth nodded his way. A glance up and down the corridor revealed no one else, so the bloke had to be motioning to Gray. Now he was crooking a finger before he headed back into his flat. Gray straightened and walked towards the open door, wondering what the hell was going on.

He could see the man making his way through the interior, using the wall for support and wheezing like a kettle. Gray stepped over the threshold.

The goth, now seated in a voluminous leather armchair, the kind usually seen in expensive offices, introduced himself as Ian Wells. "Did you close the door?"

Gray nodded. Truth be told he couldn't remember if he had or not.

"Good," said Wells. "Can't be too careful around here."

"What is it you want?"

"You smell like a copper."

"You have a good nose."

"Show us your badge, then."

Gray obliged, handing over his warrant card for Wells to examine. While he did so, Gray took in the living room. The layout was identical to Buckingham's, only the furnishings varied. A huge black television, sofa, sideboard, nest of tables, all in a dark wood. Then some models of spaceships, *Star Trek* maybe (Gray was no expert), and several bleached white animal skulls. A strong breeze whistled through the open window, the sound of traffic creeping up from below.

"Looks genuine," said Wells.

"I'm glad you think so."

"Take a seat."

"No thanks. I can't stay long."

"Sad business about the kid next door."

"Did you know him?"

"Not really. I saw him around, heard him mostly. Heard them all."

"What do you mean?"

"You're aware what that place is, right?"

"Assume I don't." Gray actually didn't.

"It's a knocking shop."

"Is that a fact?"

"I know what this tells me." Wells pointed to an ear. "I don't sleep too good, so I'm up and around a lot. And the walls are thin."

"Did you inform my colleagues of this yesterday?"

"I must have missed them. I wasn't in when it all kicked off. I only get away every Friday. A charity, Out and About, fetches me here and there. It takes me the rest of the week to recover."

"So what do you think happened?"

Wells shrugged. "How would I know? You're the copper."

"Hazard a guess."

"Unrequited love? Maybe someone fell for someone else."

"Fell? What do you mean?"

"Not in the sense of gravity but, you know, in love."

"Okay."

"Sorry. I write poetry and sometimes my sense of drama overtakes me."

"Right." Gray was keen to move on. The worst kind of writers wanted to tell you all about their work, which was the last thing he wanted to hear, particularly if it was bloody poetry. "Tell me about these noises you heard."

Wells frowned. "Are you some sort of perv?"

"Humour me."

"If you insist. Grunts, groans, that sort of thing."

"That's it?"

"What more do you want?"

"Would you be prepared to make a statement?"

"About grunts and groans?"

"About everything."

"No chance. I'm not talking openly to one of your lot. Far too dangerous."

"Why talk to me in the first place then?"

"Doesn't mean to say I don't want to help."

"Is there anything else you want to tell me?"

"Not much more to say, really. Lots of comings and goings at all times of the day and night. Different girls in there for a while, then they're gone. The same older men turning up, over and over. I see them, down below, when they leave."

"Anyone you'd recognise?"

Wells's face closed off, a shutter dropping over his eyes. "No."

"Certain?"

"Time for you to go, I think."

"Why? What are you afraid of?" Wells wouldn't meet his eye, concentrating instead on another cigarette, then staring out the window.

He looked like Gray had slapped him in the face.

Eleven

The vicarage stood adjacent to the church, within the graveyard boundary. The small windows of the brick and flint cottage overlooked the supermarket and car park to the front and the stones to the rear. Gray couldn't decide which view was more miserable.

The back door was reached via a tiny enclosed garden replete with rose bushes which burst into fragrant bloom at the height of summer, but which for now were spindly and brown.

Gray pushed at a gate constructed of a grey wood. Reverend Hill once told him it was the discards from a coffin that a previous incumbent hadn't wanted to go to waste.

Gray thumped on the door. He hadn't been here in years. He was trying to work out how long it had been when Alice Newbold opened up.

"This is a surprise, Solomon," she said.

And nobody was more surprised than Gray. What was Kate's best friend doing here? "I'm here to see Reverend Hill."

Alice opened the door and stepped back to allow him entry. "What was it about?"

"He didn't say."

Gray peered around the dim hallway. White-painted walls, some stairs, and a series of closed doors.

Alice pointed to one that led into the living room, which was plain and functional. A couple of high-backed comfortable chairs, a coffee table, and some bookshelves. The obligatory cross on the wall and a few family photographs. A dusty painting of the church. A radio on the windowsill. No television.

"Cup of tea?" Alice asked.

"No thanks."

"It's nice to have you back, Solomon."

Gray didn't know how to respond. He wasn't back per se. "Where is David?"

"He popped out."

"Will he be long?"

"I've no idea."

"Oh."

"Are you sure you don't want that cup of tea?"

"I don't want to waste your time."

"Somewhere better to be?"

Gray didn't. "Okay then, as long as you have Earl Grey."

"We have every kind of tea." Alice bustled off into the kitchen.

Through the window Gray watched the comings and goings in the supermarket across the road, wondering why David wanted to see him.

In the kitchen, china clinked, the kettle boiled, and after a while Alice returned. She carried a tray burdened with a teapot, some cups, a cream jug, a sugar bowl, and several varieties of biscuit on a plate.

She placed the tray on the low coffee table. "Four sugars, wasn't it?"

Something Gray had said years before, just to niggle her. She hadn't forgotten.

"These days it's no sugar."

"Garibaldi or Hob Nob?" Alice said, offering the biscuits. He took two out of politeness and she handed him a plate. "For the crumbs."

Once Alice had her own drink she took one of the chairs, nodding to the other for Gray. A silence descended. It wasn't uncomfortable, it was simply that neither had anything to say.

Eventually Alice broke the silence. "Do you ever think of her?"

He didn't have to ask who she meant. "Of course. Constantly."

"So do I. I miss her greatly."

Gray didn't want to enter into a competition as to who cared the most for Kate.

"Do you know why she killed herself?" asked Alice.

"How could I? She didn't leave a note or any explanation."

"She did," Alice paused. "She left me a letter."

"A letter?" Gray was so surprised, he couldn't help but repeat Alice's words. "What did it say?"

"I don't know. I burnt it. Unopened."

"What?" Gray felt as if he'd been punched in the chest by a powerful fist. He struggled to draw breath, and his heart thumped. "You didn't read it?"

"I couldn't."

"Why didn't you give it to me?"

"It wasn't addressed to you."

"Oh my God." Gray put a hand to his head. He stood, felt dizzy. "Why didn't you tell me?"

"I didn't think Kate wanted you to know. I couldn't betray her like that."

He steadied his stance, willing himself not to strangle Alice. "So why tell me now?"

She looked down to her hands. "It feels like enough time has passed."

He had to get out of here or he'd do something he regretted. He lurched towards the door.

"Don't you want to wait for Reverend Hill?"

Gray stumbled outside.

Twelve

Ten Years Ago

Gray watched Tom taking in the sights with eyes almost too wide for his head. The funfair was a perplexity of lights, sounds, and smells that were a constant enticement to the innocent.

Tom had opened his presents and cards as soon as he awoke. Kate took too many pictures, Tom complaining about being made to pose rather than run around. His sister sulked. Someone else was getting the attention the oldest child craved, but only once she realised she wasn't alone to soak up all the love. Tom went to school under duress; he wanted the funfair. And now they were here.

Gray held Tom's hand, the boy's tiny fingers enveloped within his. The entertainment was in full swing. Tom and Gray were like salmon, swimming upstream against the tide, slipping in and out of the people-current all around them. Gray clutched Tom tighter still. Everyone was looking up or ahead, unaware of the tiny six-year-old buffeted by tree-trunk legs.

"What do you want to do first?" asked Gray.

"Ghost train!"

Gray shook his head. Tom's bottom lip protruded far enough to hang a coat off it. "Let's get you some candy floss." The pout withdrew.

Sugar feathered onto the stick in an ever-widening whorl until it was the size of Tom's head. A young woman with tattoos and earrings swapped the sugar rush on a stick for some coins. They walked while Tom ate.

Next stop was hook-a-duck. It took Tom a little time to catch one of the floating chunks of yellow plastic. He pointed at a goldfish. The short bloke behind the counter coughed, spat, held up three stubby fingers. That was how many ducks Tom would need to snag. Three meant lots of money.

"We'll be almost out of cash," said Gray to Tom. He'd rushed out of the house without checking his wallet. Just the change in his pocket. Not enough.

"Fish!"

"Okay."

Gray nodded at the guy, handed over the coins. The money disappeared into a pocket. As predicted, Gray was pretty much done. During Tom's fishing expedition he felt uncomfortable, as if someone was watching. Gray turned, scanned the crowd. There were people everywhere. None looking in their direction. Gray shook his head. Stupid. He placed a protective hand on Tom's shoulder nevertheless.

Tom snagged the final duck and let out a little cheer. The man lifted down a fish in a bag of water. Handed it over. It didn't seem very golden. Pretty anaemic. Tom took Gray's hand again.

"Time to go home," said Gray.

"Ghost train!" Tom threw a minor paddy when Gray told him no.

And then, stupidly, Gray relented.

Thirteen

"How was the rest of your weekend, Sol?" asked Hamson.

She lurked in a corner of the detectives' office which some years ago had received a TV-style makeover (i.e. cheap and fast) into an improvised kitchen by the addition of a small strip of Formica, now chipped and scratched into oblivion. A dirty kettle, a half-empty jar of coffee, some scrunched tea bags, lumpy sugar, and stained cutlery completed the portrait. The team were pushing for a microwave and a fridge. Carslake wouldn't have it, concerned the stench of zapped curry and decomposing French cheese would become a permanent fixture.

Hamson stirred her coffee, clinking the spoon against the ceramic cup with each revolution. A pause, and then the next vessel received a similar battering by the tarnished metal utensil. It put Gray's teeth on edge; made his head hurt more than usual.

He was about to complain when Hamson halted her assault and picked up the mugs. She walked over to his desk, heels clicking on the linoleum.

"After you called, I was in here for half of it." Gray shrugged. "The weather was lousy for the rest. To be honest, I'm glad to be back at work."

"Among the dead and dying."

"And you." There was a momentary pause, Hamson unresponsive, motionless except for her eyes as a uniform walked through the office, her Medusa-like gaze upon him. "Von, am I going to get my drink before it goes cold?"

"Sorry, I'm all over the place today." Hamson stretched out an arm.

"What's new?" Gray accepted the mug, holding it around the circumference. It was scalding. He placed the mug on the desk, spilling some coffee in the process, and blew on his fingers. "Bloody hell, are you trying to hospitalise me?"

Heads looked up from desks, saw it was Gray shouting, then shook it off and went back to work. The usual spectacle, nothing new.

"You know what, Sol? You're a whinging bastard." Hamson, who always gave as good as she got, adopted a whiny voice, "It's too cold, it's not strong enough. It's instant, not filter. Give it to me before it gets cold. Now it's too hot. Grow a pair, man."

Gray was stunned for a moment, then he burst out laughing. "That's not what I sound like, is it?"

"You're bloody impossible. Get a grip, Sergeant."

"Yes, Ma'am." Gray tugged his forelock a couple of times.

Point made, Hamson retreated to her desk tucked against the wall, messy with its own overflowing caseload and backed-up paperwork. If the police force were a U-bend it would have been beyond the rescue of a plunger years ago.

"And sorry for shouting," said Gray, not meaning it. He took a tentative sip of his boiling coffee, feeling his inspector's eyes on him. "Good, that." Two lies in as many seconds.

It tasted awful, twice-boiled water from the bottom of the kettle and instant granules that hadn't quite dissolved. Though

Gray wasn't about to say so out loud. Instead he resolved to pour it down the sink the moment Hamson wasn't looking.

Hamson applied a dash more lipstick, using a vanity mirror to get the enhancement just right. Finally, she primped her hair. Straight a couple of days ago, curly now. The colour changed regularly too.

Once finished, she turned her attention to Gray. "So what was all that crap about?"

"Actually, I ended up back at the flat."

Hamson narrowed her eyes, twisted back and gave Gray her full attention. "Why?"

"Something you said. About the suicide being just a kid. It made me think."

Hamson pulled a pained face, though avoided making a direct comment. "And?"

"Not much, really. Nothing inside, though I did speak to one of the neighbours. An Ian Wells. He said the place was a brothel." His voice petered out. "I don't know, Von. Something doesn't feel right. I just can't put my finger on it."

"It would be an explanation for all the fingerprints we found."

A non-committal grunt from Gray. He wasn't convinced either way.

"You're forgiven, by the way."

"For what?" Gray couldn't think what he might have done.

"Bitching at me."

"Oh, that."

"Do it again and I'll uninvite you to my birthday night out."

Gray regretted his earlier apology. It could have been a way out of the dreaded piss-up. He wasn't interested in attending Hamson's celebrations, but she kept going on about it and deep down he knew he'd probably end up going.

Hamson absorbed Gray's less-than-enthusiastic response. Gray employed a common avoidance tactic and grabbed his desk phone. With the dial tone droning in his ear he searched for the number of the social worker, Rosemary Dent.

The notepad he'd written the details on had become buried over the previous thirty-six hours while someone else used his desk. He found the pad, flipped back a few pages until he saw his own scrawl.

He reset the line, which had begun to wail at him in protest at being unused for too long, and rattled in the numbers, avoiding Hamson's glare. She'd give up soon, distracted by her caseload. This time the phone rang through.

Dent answered with her name. Gray responded with his. She didn't mess around and got straight to the point. That, and the rapidity of her speech, gave the hearty impression of a person with precious little time to spare.

"What can I do for you, Sergeant? I'm about to go out into the field."

"Sounds like you're FBI, Mrs Dent."

"It's Ms."

Two can play at that game.

He adopted an identical cut and thrust approach. "Nick Buckingham. He was one of yours, I believe?"

Dent's voice immediately warmed, her manner shifting from officious to self-congratulatory. "He most certainly was, and a resounding success, I might add."

"I'm sorry to tell you he's dead."

"That's awful!" said Dent. Gray let the silence stretch until she asked, "What were the circumstances?"

"Suicide is suspected."

"Oh my. That doesn't sound like Nick at all, he's a survivor. What happened?"

"We're still investigating, Miss Dent, so I'm afraid I can't share all the details, although I expect there will be a coroner's enquiry in the near future."

"Which station did you say you were from?"

"Margate, on the Kent coast."

"I know where it is, Sergeant. You'd be amazed how many of my charges end up there."

"I wouldn't be surprised at all. I see it daily."

"Quite."

"Can you tell me about him? I just need the brief details. For background, you understand."

"Of course." Dent launched into a rapid-fire speech on Buckingham's history, which added little to what Gray already knew. It was a sorry tale of rejection and desolation. Ultimately there were the beginnings of possible rehabilitation, initiated by his arrest in Green Park.

"I was so convinced we'd straightened him out. I can't believe he killed himself."

"His records state he was passed to you as a condition of his sentence, right?"

"Yes, but it wasn't for long. We found Nick a stable home, he seemed much happier."

"And that was it?"

"Pretty much."

"You didn't see him regularly?"

"Not after I handed on his case. Why would I?"

"Is that normal?"

"Entirely." Dent's tone hardened again. "My turn to ask the questions, Sergeant. Where did you get my name?"

"The care notes. And I spoke to DC Yandell on Saturday."

"I remember him. He was a bit aggressive. I much preferred his colleague. Pennance? Nice man."

"And you had no idea Nick had moved down here?"

"I'm afraid not. As I said, he was rehoused and left my jurisdiction."

"He never mentioned Margate?"

"No."

"Why would he be here then?"

"I've really no idea, Sergeant. Although I could give you one theory."

"Okay."

"I could be completely wrong, of course."

"I won't hold it against you, Miss Dent."

"Sometimes adopted children develop an overwhelming urge to find their parents."

Gray's stomach plunged. "Excuse me?"

"Adoptees. On occasion they want to know where they come from."

"You're not sure, though?"

"It's as good a reason as any, isn't it?"

Gray had one more question, but he couldn't ask it. He thanked Dent with more enthusiasm than before, and terminated the call. He sat back and thought about what she'd said.

Sometimes children get an overwhelming urge to find their parents...

Gray's mobile rang. Absently, he answered.

A voice he recognised said, "I understand you have a corpse on your hands."

"Where the hell have you been?"

"That's no way to talk to a superior officer," said Detective Inspector Marcus Pennance.

Fourteen

D I Pennance worked in the Sapphire unit of the Metropolitan Police, the section responsible for serious sexual crimes and child protection. Their paths had crossed a few years ago thanks to a report of a kid found in London that sounded like it might be Tom. Gray got in touch with Pennance via a friend of a friend. Pennance had done what he could (which, ultimately, wasn't anything) and asked for a favour in return. Buckingham was just one more deed in a long list, though this time he was on Gray's doorstep.

"Are you somewhere private?" asked Pennance.

"No, but I can be."

"I'll call you on your mobile in two minutes."

Gray disconnected, scooped up his mobile, headed out of the office and to the incident room. He stuck his head around the door. It was empty. Gray took the meeting room on the left, closed the door behind him. It wouldn't appear unusual, him taking some privacy here. He paced the floor while he waited for Pennance to call, answering the instant his phone rang.

"What the bloody hell have you got me into? And where have you been?"

"I've been busy."

"And all the while I've been up to my neck in it here, thanks to you. My number was on Buckingham's fucking mobile. I've got my DI and DCI all over me!"

"It's done. You could have just told me to piss off."

"And you could have told me everything," said Gray.

"Did you really want to know?" Pennance shot back.

That made him pause. Pennance was right, even though Gray wasn't about to admit it. He certainly wanted to know now. Everything.

He said so.

"I can't tell you too much over the phone, of course. Buckingham was involved."

"How?"

"He was integral to building a prosecution against some powerful people."

"And now he's dead."

"Yes."

"As a direct result of your work?"

"I don't know. It's possible."

"He was the same age as my son, for God's sake."

"I'm well aware of his age."

"Why wasn't I?"

"Because you would have asked questions I couldn't answer."

"Too right I would have done. You kept me in the dark. You used me."

"I didn't plan on Buckingham getting himself killed."

"Bad judgement on your part, then."

Pennance sighed down the phone. His next words sounded more contrite. "I never wanted any of this to happen. It was supposed to be simple. Just somewhere for Buckingham to stay for a while. I want to make this right. I want to come down and investigate Nick's death properly."

"Why not just put a request in?"

"I have."

"So what's the problem?"

"Your Chief Inspector."

"Carslake?"

"That's the one. He's resisting."

Something here didn't make sense to Gray. "I don't get it."

"I can't go telling everyone what's underway, it would seriously jeopardise my enquiries."

"Why me?"

"We both know you're the sort of man who'd understand my objectives and want to help without too many questions asked."

Pennance operated both sides of the law, used his position to get to offenders the police couldn't touch. Paedophiles in particular. Pennance ran a tiny discrete unit who transmitted vital information onto a more visible civilian group, which then went after those evading the law. Gray had become part of it, as a result of his involvement with Pennance when looking for Tom.

"It feels like you're using me again."

"Yes, but for a very good reason. I'm sure you'll understand once we get the chance to speak face to face."

"So until then, I remain in the dark?"

"Out of necessity."

Gray didn't like this one little bit. Pennance was astute enough to know how to manipulate him.

"You're asking me to talk to Carslake for you?"

"Yes. Vouch for me. Make him feel at ease with the idea of my presence."

Gray wasn't happy. He knew the questions from his superiors about his mobile number wouldn't stop. And he knew his own mind wouldn't stop asking whether Nick was really Tom.

Pennance was a man who looked after himself. Perhaps it would be better to have him here, under Gray's nose, rather than miles away in the capital and under someone else's.

"Now, Sergeant, are you going to speak to your DCI for me?"

"Against my better judgement, yes."

"Good man. I'll be in touch when you get me the go-ahead."

Gray disconnected. Massaged his temples. He could feel a headache starting.

Fifteen

On Gray's return to the detectives' office he stopped at Fowler's desk. "Any information about who owns the flat yet?"

"No."

"Bit slow, aren't we, Mike?"

"Have you seen my workload?" Fowler pointed to a pile of folders and paperwork big enough to need oxygen at its peak. "I'm off down to the Jobcentre offices later on this morning, though."

"Good. What about the fingerprints on the glass?"

"Two sets of dabs were found. One was Buckingham's and some partials around the rim. Unidentified, though."

Gray thought about that. Someone had lifted the glass at the top.

"Okay, let me know as soon as you learn something."

"Your wish is my command."

Box ticked, Gray turned away.

"Everything all right?" said Hamson. "You look like someone's kicked you in the balls."

Before Gray could respond, Carslake leant into the office and nodded his head at him to follow. Hamson gave Gray a questioning look. He responded in kind, even though he had a pretty good idea what was going on.

"What's the matter?" said Gray when he was in the corridor.

"Not until we're upstairs," snapped Carslake.

Swimming in the DCI's wake, Gray considered what he should say. By the time he was on the top floor he wasn't any the wiser and scarcely registered the usual deadly glare from Sylvia.

Barely had Carslake closed the door when he barked, "Sit down." Gray did as he was told, while Carslake stalked his desk like a praying mantis, stiff with anger. He leant on the wood, his jaw set. "Have you been speaking to the Met?"

"The Met?"

"Are you bloody deaf?"

Gray opted to tell the truth, most of it at least, and rise above Carslake's petulance. "Briefly, on Saturday. I spoke to a PC Yandell. It was about the Buckingham suicide. Why, what's happened?"

"You've created quite a stir, that's what. They want to send one of their men down, a DI Pennance. I've just had the third call about it from Superintendent Marsh."

"Bloody hell."

"Quite. There's something about this Buckingham kid that's rattled a few cages, thanks to you."

"How was I supposed to know this would happen?"

"You've worked on the force long enough to know that poking around outside your jurisdiction creates waves, particularly when it comes to those cockney buggers. Well, haven't you?"

"Sorry."

Carslake let out a deep sigh and said, "You're a bloody idiot, do you know that?"

"Yes, sir."

The DCI's backside hit the chair hard. He fell into a stony silence. Gray let the man calm down. "What's done is done. Next time, come to me." Gray nodded. Carslake was seemingly mollified, the threatened storm just a squall and already blown out. "I pulled a few strings at HQ, got his specifics emailed over to me. I had Sylvia print it out. I know how much you prefer a hard copy."

Carslake held out a manila folder. It was fairly thick, so he was no rookie, this one. Plenty of time to build up a list of misdemeanours or, worse, successes. Gray knew all about Pennance, though Carslake wasn't to know that.

"The boy comes with a pretty good record," said Carslake. "Keen as mustard. Definitely one destined for greatness."

"I love the sound of that."

"That's what worries me. Perhaps he's after his next leg up."

The file housed a litany of positive reports and arrests. Even so, one incident stood out. A father had gone for his step kid with a knife after stabbing the mother. Armed response was five minutes away so Pennance took down the guy single-handedly, saved the kid's life. Fearless, his commanding officer stated. Gray could think of other, less flattering descriptions.

"That caught my eye, too," said Carslake.

"It says here Pennance got passed over for a commendation because he gave the father a right royal pasting."

"His single blemish. It's probably the least the bastard deserved, between you and me. Something bothers me, Sol. A few days ago this was a straightforward suicide, now there's some out-of-towner crawling all over it. Why?"

"Beats me." Gray dropped the folder on the desk, keen to end the discussion on Pennance. "It'll come out in time Jeff. Always does."

Carslake sighed. "I guess you're right. Anything from Clough on the post-mortem results?"

"I haven't heard from him. Buckingham is low priority I'd imagine."

"Not any more. Give him a kick up the backside, would you? If that doesn't work, tell me and I'll give him one myself."

"Of course, sir." Carslake looked like he'd relish the chance to boot Clough.

"The Super's left it up to me to decide whether this Pennance works with us or not."

"Trust him to pass the buck."

"That's the benefit of rank. Speaking of which, what do you think?"

"I say we bring him down here. Maybe he'll be able to help. Think of it as free resource. He'll support our clearance rate."

"Screw the clearance rate. It's Sapphire. Everything they deal with is distasteful." Gray said nothing. "You understand if this all goes tits up, it's my responsibility?"

"Yes."

"Good, because if it happens, I won't be the only one looking at an early pension."

"Understood."

"I'll call the Super."

"I think it's the right thing to do."

A grunt from Carslake preceded his words: "Doesn't mean it's best, though. Let's just get him in and out of here as quickly as possible."

Gray made to get up.

"Sit back down, I haven't finished with you yet. The Super isn't happy for another reason."

"Is he ever?"

"When it comes to you, no. Brian Blake has been on at him. He complained about your negligent behaviour, as he put it, with regard to the Buckingham investigation."

"That's a load of crap, and you know it, sir."

"As does the Super. We still have to make it up to him, though. Doesn't do well to rattle the boss's cage."

"Can I do a few Hail Marys instead?"

"Wrong religion."

"Shouldn't this be down to DI Hamson? She's my commanding officer, after all."

"She's not the one who's a walking cock-up, so you'll be DI Pennance's liaison. Makes sense as you were at the suicide."

"Only briefly."

"And that was Blake's point."

"DI Hamson won't be happy."

"Let me deal with her."

"When do I get Pennance, then?"

"Once I give the go-ahead, he's on a train. Probably tomorrow morning. We'll put him up at a hotel down the road. The one by the station, whatever it's called. Sylvia will know."

Gray waved the folder. "Can I have this?"

"It's all yours. And keep me up to date. I don't like this."

"Neither do I."

GRAY LEANED OVER HAMSON'S desk. "Have you got any ciggies with you?"

"I thought you'd given up."

"I've decided to un-give up."

"That's not even a word."

"It is now. Come on, outside."

"Who gives the orders round here?"

"Your guess is as good as mine, Von."

The pair stood alone in the car park. The tang of engine oil from the array of parked vehicles merged with the odour of fried food vented by the pub next door. It made for a heady mixture about to be contaminated further by cigarette smoke.

After taking one for herself, Hamson put the pack away.

"I'll take one," said Gray. Surprised, Hamson drew the pack out again and handed it over.

Gray extracted a cigarette and clamped it between his lips. He'd not touched one for two years. Hamson lit hers, passed the lighter over. Gray thumbed the wheel; the flame caught. Gray sucked on the filter, drew the smoke into the back of his throat. The cloud scraped its way down his gullet and entered his lungs. Gray coughed.

It was like the first time all over again. The rough taste, him wondering why the hell he was subjecting his body to this. But he took another hit and then it was just like he remembered. Why the hell had he given up?

Hamson watched Gray with amusement. The pair enjoyed half a cigarette before Hamson spoke. "What's going on, Sol?"

"People keep asking me that. I haven't got a bloody clue, but I've just had a DI landed on me." Gray passed her Pennance's personnel file. She flicked it open and glanced through the contents. She brightened at Pennance's photo, frowned when she absorbed the detail.

"Why you?" she said.

"Apparently, I've upset Superintendent Marsh and Carslake again, so this is atonement. I thought I'd give you a heads-up before the DCI has a word."

"Bloody Carslake. Chauvinist."

"Which is why I wanted to warn you, he wouldn't react well to an accusation like that."

"It's the truth."

"Maybe, but he's still the boss." Gray remembered Carslake's earlier comment - this job was all about keeping the boss happy.

Hamson hissed smoke through her teeth, shook her head. "The Met, though. What's that all about?"

Gray crossed his fingers behind his back. "You know as much as I do, Von. Anyway, he'll have to wait for now. I've got an appointment."

Sixteen

"Edward Festival?"

The battle-hardened, grey-haired receptionist cast an imperious gaze over her glasses, regarding the small cluster of people seated before her, over which she wielded the ultimate power. That of access.

Mr Festival, the lucky recipient of the golden ticket, jerked into life and made his way towards his appointment.

While others idly flicked through magazines and suffered their lot within the plush, hushed surroundings, Gray grew increasingly irritated as the second hand flicked around the face of his watch at an agonisingly slow pace. He'd been kept twenty minutes over the appointment time already. This was supposed to be a private clinic, not the NHS. He got up to enquire of Dr Mallory's gatekeeper how much longer it was likely to be. Her chilly response was that he should just wait.

Gray sat back down, swore under his breath. An old boy to his left passed him a magazine. *Top Gear*. He couldn't think of anything worse.

"Read it," said the man.

Just as Gray relented and flicked open the front cover his name was called out.

"Works every time," said the old boy.

Gray passed back the magazine and got to his feet.

"Consultation room three."

Gray glanced around, uncertain where he was supposed to go. With the condescending stab of a finger and a practised, entirely audible huff the receptionist pointed to the corridor on the far side of the waiting room.

He threaded his way through the rows of waiting patients and down the passage. A short distance along was consultation room three. Along with the number, a sign read, "Out of politeness, knock first."

Gray twisted the door handle and stepped inside. He took in certificates mounted on the wall beside tasteful artwork, medical journals lined up neatly on shelves. All very different to a standard GP's office.

A besuited man sat at a large desk with his back to the entrance, hunched over his desk, scribbling away. He tossed his pen down and spun around at Gray's interruption. He was a short, tubby man with watery eyes. He looked ill himself.

"Did you not observe my note on the door?" said Mallory.

"Yes."

"And?"

"You didn't say please."

Mallory stared hard at Gray and jotted on his pad. "Take a seat." Gray closed the door and did as he was bid. "Now, what seems to be the problem?" The doctor's tone was soured cream.

"Nothing. I'm absolutely fine."

Mallory blinked, whether because of Gray's response or the state of his own eyes, it was hard to tell. "I hear something different from your Occupational Health Department."

Gray shrugged.

"You don't agree?" said Mallory.

"I'm under orders to be here."

"I see." Mallory made a further notation. "I was just reviewing your file. I see my predecessor, Doctor Stone, prescribed anti-depressants."

"Yes."

"And?"

Gray was pleased to detect frustration in the doctor's voice. "I stopped taking them."

"Why?"

"They ran out and I didn't need them anymore. I still don't."

Mallory sat back and steepled his fingers. He regarded Gray for a few moments and Gray stared blankly back.

"Sleeping all right?"

"Reasonable, thanks."

"All the way through the night?"

"More or less."

"Which?"

Gray didn't reply. He knew it was childish to needle the man. A warmer bedside manner wouldn't go amiss, though.

"We can do this the easy way or the hard way. Isn't that what policeman say on television?" said Mallory.

"The made-up ones."

"Fictional or not, your commanding officer is awaiting my report. It's my call as to whether you take an enforced leave. Or not."

"I've got too much work to take time off."

"Then play the game, Sergeant."

They glared at each other. Gray blinked first. He needed to keep busy. Both he and Mallory knew it. "Okay."

"Let's have a look at your blood pressure." Mallory dragged a rectangular black box across his desk, flipped it open and started assembling the equipment. "Roll up your sleeve, please."

"That's not necessary."

"I thought we'd just covered this? I have to do a basic examination before I can decide what action to take. Now please do as I've asked."

Gray removed his jacket, undid the cuff and rolled up the sleeve. Mallory wrapped the black band around Gray's arm and set the machine going. The band constricted. Gray didn't like these examinations, he always thought the device would just keep squeezing and squeezing until it burst muscle, breached sinew and met bone. As usual the device stopped when the tightness was becoming uncomfortable, emitting a penetrating beep.

The doctor pursed his lips and made a further illegible scribble.

"Is everything all right?" Gray couldn't help himself.

"Open your shirt, please."

Gray loosened his tie, undid the first three buttons and held the fabric open while Mallory applied a stethoscope to first his chest and then his back.

"You could have warmed it first."

"I only do that for the children. Can't abide them bawling."

Scooting the scope around Gray's rib cage, Mallory asked him to breathe in and out a few times.

"You can do yourself back up now."

While Gray rearranged his clothing the doctor scratched at his pad. As Gray knotted his tie the doctor lifted his ophthalmoscope and held it out like a weapon.

"I'm just going to take a look into your eyes."

Without pause Mallory shone a tight beam of light into Gray's left, then right pupil.

"All done?" Gray blinked several times.

"Yes," replied Mallory, sitting back in his chair.

Gray shrugged his jacket back on. "So I've got the all-clear then?"

"No."

Gray paused, his fingers poised over a shirt button.

"You're a policeman, which is a high-pressure job."

"Everyone experiences stress to a certain degree."

"Has anything happened at work recently?"

"Not that I can think of."

"Are you sure?"

"I don't think so. Why?"

"Both your blood pressure and heart rate are significantly higher than your last recorded check-up, which, to be frank, was far too long ago. In addition to that, your pupils are dilated, you appear tense, and I think it is fair to say that you are irritable."

"No more than usual."

Mallory smiled thinly. "That's as may be, but you can't tell me you're feeling normal. Otherwise your commanding officer wouldn't have seen fit to send you in."

"What's normal?"

"Quite."

"So you're saying I'm subconsciously seeking help?"

"Yes."

"That's ridiculous."

Mallory spread his hands wide. "Then why are you here?"

"Because Carslake insisted!"

"How's everything at home?"

Gray was caught off guard by the sudden change in tack. "Fine. I've plenty on the go."

"Out of the office?"

"The garden is a constant challenge."

"Where did your daughter move to?"

"Why is this relevant?" Gray clenched his fists, dug his nails into his palms.

"Just answer the question."

"Initially she went to live with her grandparents. Now? I've no idea. She might still be there. I never hear from Hope these days."

"She's not been in contact since she left?"

"No." It had been five years.

"And how long since your wife passed away?"

The heat within Gray rose another notch. Through gritted teeth he said, "She didn't pass away. She committed suicide."

"Is that an important distinction?"

"No."

"Then why mention it?"

"I don't know! Why all these fucking questions?"

Mallory sat back in his chair, considered Gray for a few moments while he calmed down.

"Sorry," said Gray. "That was uncalled for."

"There's no need to apologise." Mallory's tone was softer. "You ought to consider counselling."

"Yeah, right."

"You need help, Solomon. I see you refused to consider it at the time, and I suspect all you've done since is bottle things up."

"That's not true." Gray thought of Pennance and the case files at home. "I've been proactive."

"Good."

"And they were different times back then. The police wasn't the touchy-feely thing it is now. We were expected to get on with it. We still are."

"Nevertheless, I'm going to recommend you see Doctor Ichan. She's an excellent therapist."

"I don't need one."

"She's very professional."

"I already said no."

"In that case, I agree with you."

"What do you mean?"

"You shouldn't be on those pills."

"Thank Christ for that."

Mallory picked up his pen and scribbled away at a prescription pad. A moment later he tore off the page and flourished it at Gray.

Gray took the sheet, glanced over it. "You're giving me something else?"

"Yes. You need help. If you refuse counselling, medication is the only other option. Be warned. It'll be about three weeks before you feel their full effect and your moods may cycle in between."

Gray sat, still holding the prescription, the unverified threat hanging in the air.

It's my call whether you take an enforced leave. Or not.

"I need to work."

"Yes, I suspect you do. So would you like to see Doctor Ichan instead?"

Gray nodded.

"Expect a letter in about a week's time confirming your appointment. And I want to see you again in a month. Make an appointment on your way out. Any problems, call me."

Mallory pulled a keyboard towards him and started to tap away. Gray had no choice but to take the unsubtle hint.

"Could you close the door behind you?" said Mallory, still focused on his computer screen. "Please."

Gray did as he was told, feeling like a contrite schoolboy leaving the headmaster's office. He looked once more at the prescription and then stuffed it into his jacket pocket.

"Bloody overpaid quacks," he said.

Gray ignored the receptionist as he strode out of the surgery and into the sunlight.

THE KEY GRATED IN THE Yale lock. Gray fetched several shopping bags from the doorstep into the hallway. He then brought the rest of the produce into the house from the car and pushed the door shut with his foot.

He lugged his purchases into the narrow kitchen, all pretty basic stuff – ready meals, pies, a few frozen vegetables that could be microwaved, and some single pieces of fruit. Most of it was on offer, which had been the primary influence on Gray's selections.

The last item Gray unpacked was Mallory's prescription. He'd handed the paper in at the beginning of the shopping trip and collected the medication at the end, just as the chemist was closing up.

Gray placed the innocuous-looking container on the counter. He bent over and stared through the brown plastic. He'd taken various chemicals for depression and anxiety over the years and honestly believed he was past all that. He was pissed off to discover he wasn't.

He picked up the bottle, began to unscrew the cap, then put it back down. Using the pills would be an admission of a problem, one Mallory had rightly observed he had always refused to talk about. He wasn't about to now, either.

There'd be no giving in. He'd handle this himself, his way. And lie to everyone in the process. Gray tossed the bottle into a drawer. Of course, Carslake would check up on him; that was one hundred percent certain. Gray needed to carry the pills around for show. He took a couple of the pills out of the bottle and threw them into the bin. It would give the appearance he'd been consuming them.

A ready meal got its just desserts in the microwave, zapped for five-and-a-half minutes until it was, as the packaging put it, piping hot throughout. Gray poured a beer, placed crockery, glass and utensils onto a tray and lugged everything upstairs to his bedroom, three flights of stairs away.

The tray went onto a desk shoved in a corner, pushing the computer keyboard out of the way first. He flicked on the fan heater and it whirred into life. Gray pulled over the folder of information he'd printed out earlier and stuck a label on the front, writing on it, *Buckingham, Nick*.

As the first forkful of food entered his mouth Gray began to read.

Seventeen

In the reception area, Gray took Pennance in at a glance. Good-looking, well-dressed, and well-groomed. He looked mid-thirties, but likely to be a decade older given the rank. It was hard to tell. He probably used expensive anti-ageing creams, worked out five times a week and only drank mineral water. The picture of a modern man. No wedding ring.

"Good to see you again, DS Gray." Pennance stepped away from the front desk and held out his hand. The handshake was dry and on the right side of firm. His expression conveyed a serious, business-like attitude.

"Been a while." Gray had mostly dealt with him over email, occasionally via the phone, and only once face to face, when Gray had headed to London to follow up on the lead regarding Tom.

"I'm just keen to get going. Thanks for accommodating me at such short notice."

"Not a problem." It was. "What precisely is it you want to get going on?"

Pennance shook his head. "You know I can't. Not here."

"Come on through. I'll show you around." Gray jerked a thumb at the desk sergeant, who leant beneath the desk and pressed a release switch. The door unlocked with a distinct click.

Gray led Pennance from the public area into the back office, along maze-like corridors and to the door marked CID.
He opened it to reveal the jumble of desks, chairs and phones.
Usually it was a hive of activity. At the moment it was embar-
rassingly quiet, and the three residents bore expressions that
ranged from expectant (Hamson) to suspicious (Fowler).

Fowler tugged at his moustache, kettle poised over a couple
of cups.

"Is this him?" Fowler asked Gray.

Pennance answered. "If you mean, am I DI Pennance?
Then yes."

"I suppose you'll be wanting a coffee."

"Just some water if you have it."

"Plenty round here. You've got a choice of source, though."

"Excuse me?"

"The sea or the toilets."

Gray smiled inside. Pennance's face didn't move a millime-
tre.

"The comedian here is DS Mike Fowler," said Gray. Fowler
raised his mug in a greeting.

"I'm DI Yvonne Hamson." Hamson left the confines of her
desk to cross the floor. Then she enveloped Pennance's hand in
both of hers and shook it. "Nice to meet you. And don't listen
to Mike. We have a water cooler. I'll gladly get you some."

"Be careful there, mate," said Fowler to Pennance as Hamson departed.

"Ignore him," said Gray.

"You don't sound much like a cockney," said Fowler. "Your
accent. No apples and pears in it, is there, Sol?"

Gray shook his head at Fowler. They'd be having words later.

"That's because I'm from Hampshire." Pennance smiled. "I've moved around a lot over the years. Home is where the job is. Currently London, temporarily Margate."

It was a neat speech. Pennance had probably delivered it many times.

"Here's your water," said Hamson on re-entry. In her hand was a clear plastic cup. Condensation mottled the exterior.

"Thank you."

"Kiss-arse," said Fowler, which won him a glare from Hamson. He took his coffee to his desk and started hammering away at a keyboard.

"I presume this is our guest?" Carslake filled the doorway, friendly in a grandfatherly way. He introduced himself, took Pennance's hand and vigorously shook it. His arm was probably beginning to ache, given the amount of attention it was getting.

"Delighted you could make it. Good journey?" said Carslake.

"Not bad. Slow from Ashford onwards."

"We're a bit out in the sticks here, I'm afraid."

"The rest of the team will be in shortly. You can meet them all then," said Gray.

"Had anything to eat yet?" asked Carslake.

"I grabbed some toast on the train."

Fowler pulled a face over his shoulder, interested again now Carslake was on the scene. "I bet that was a disgusting experience. Bacon and eggs, that's what you need. Put some meat on your bones."

"Sounds good," said Gray.

"For once I have to agree with the DS here," said Carslake. Gray wondered which one of them he was referring to. "Come on, there's a half-decent café round the corner, does an all-day breakfast."

"I'm fine," said Pennance. "I'd just like to get into it."

"I'm sure your case can wait a few minutes." Carslake wouldn't be denied when food came into the equation.

Pennance gave in. "I guess so, sir."

Eighteen

Ten Years Ago

It was late by the time Gray got home. Dark, the curtains tightly drawn, the street lights casting their amber hue. The front door was unlocked.

"She's still out," said Alice, framed in the entrance to the living room. "She's looking for him."

Alice's expression said, *Why aren't you?*

Gray liked Alice, but wasn't keen on her influence over Kate. The women were friends through church. Alice, however, was a zealot. No arguing with God's word. Gray was convinced Alice preached her husband, a quiet man, into an early grave.

Gray once jokingly told Kate he'd open a cold case, get the corpse exhumed and check for foul play. As it turned out, the only thing foul about the situation was Kate's mood thereafter.

"Why are you here?" asked Gray.

"Someone has to look after little Hope," said Alice. "Would you rather she was left alone?"

Gray couldn't bear the thought of Alice's unwavering, biblical devotion extending to Hope, even if she was asleep. But he chose to keep quiet and thus keep the peace.

Alice said, "I'll make us a cup of tea." She stepped into the kitchen, began the process of boiling water and getting cups down. Gray trailed in her wake. Alice always behaved as if she belonged here, as if this was her house. Gray decided he needed something stronger than tea. He found it in a cupboard in the dining room.

A quarter of the whisky bottle was drained by the time Alice brought through the china-laden tray. She pursed her lips when she caught sight of Gray, slumped in a chair, bottle in hand. He responded by pouring himself a drink, draining it, and following up with another.

Alice placed the tray on the table, laid out two cups. Sending the message that Gray *would* be drinking tea.

"You should be out there too," she said.

"My colleagues are searching high and low. And I'm here for Hope."

"As you were for Tom?" Alice held out a cup balanced on a saucer. "One sugar or two?"

"Four."

Four spoonfuls entered the tea. A teaspoon rattled. The cup was passed over again. Gray took it, swallowed. Ignored the burn and the sickly sweet taste. He raised the cup in a salute.

"You can leave now," said Gray.

"I don't think so. Your wife also needs looking after."

"That's my job."

"Your *job* is precisely the problem, Solomon."

Gray stood, swayed, tried to hide it, and lurched forward. "Get out."

"No."

The front door opened and Kate entered. Her hair was tied back into a tight ponytail. Her eyes were puffy and shot through with red veins, the pockets beneath black shadows. She'd been crying.

Kate looked at them both - a glare for Gray, a helpless glance for Alice. Kate walked over, took the glass from Gray's hand, drained it in one. Held it out for another. Gray poured. Alice did not seem to mind when it was Kate drinking.

When the glass was empty, she put it to her cheek for a moment then dropped it. She slapped her husband hard on the face. Again. And again.

"Why? Why?" she screamed.

Gray didn't have an answer so he said nothing, accepted the beating. It was the least he could do.

Kate sank to the floor like a marionette with its strings cut, bent double, head in hands. She sobbed. He wanted to lean down and touch her, but he was drained of all emotion, still in utter shock. Only now did Alice move. She sat next to her friend and put a comforting arm around her.

Gray watched Kate sob for what seemed an age until she burned out, the depths of her soul scraped dry. Eventually she picked herself up, loped across the room.

She said over her shoulder, "I hate you."

Gray agreed. He did too.

Nineteen

Gray strode along the Margate seafront, downhill from the station. The others had driven, even though it was no more than a ten-minute saunter. He suspected Pennance would have preferred to walk also; however, Carslake had pressed him into his car, presumably to find out what the hell he was doing here.

Cars raced by in both directions, drowning out the sound of the sea. Although it was after the school rush hour the highway was still well populated. It seemed to be a fact of life now. Even the smallest of roads was overburdened with vehicles that got larger every year, all driven with less and less regard for the law.

This desire for a parent to possess a huge 4x4, just to get the little buggers to school, what was that all about?

Gray was pleased to reach Café Tanya in one piece. He shoved the door which set a brass bell jingling and stepped inside. The quartet of Carslake, Fowler, Hamson and Pennance were at a table against a wall.

The interior was airy and bright thanks to the various mirrors that covered the walls. The tables, chairs, cutlery and ceramics were all mismatched. It gave the place a quirky, lived-in atmosphere.

"We've ordered already," said Carslake.

"Did you get anything for me?"

"No idea what you wanted," said Fowler, grinning

The queue, already long enough, had just added another person. "Great."

"Should have got here sooner, Sol," said Carslake.

Bunch of arseholes.

Gray sighed and joined the line being served by Tanya Small, the slim, dark-haired woman who owned the café. Her black bob framed intense green eyes above a button nose and a very kissable pair of lips.

The smell of frying bacon wafted out from the kitchen and set Gray's stomach rumbling. He'd recently started visiting the café every work morning. The place was near the station but far enough to get some space. He tended to order the same items. The coffee in particular was good. Although the food was more expensive than those in the subsidised canteen at the station, it was much tastier. And the company was an improvement too.

Gray finally reached the front of the queue. Typically, no one else had entered after him. For once Gray didn't mind his bad luck. It meant he had the proprietor all to himself.

"Hello again," she said with a smile.

"Hi." He grinned back.

"Scrambled eggs and a flat white, as usual?"

Gray blinked. "As usual" implied familiarity. Tanya was looking to him for an answer. "Yes please," he managed.

"And what about something for lunch while you're here?"

"Yes."

"Ham and cheese baguette with pickle?" asked Tanya.

"Please."

"You can sit down if you like. I'll bring everything over when it's ready."

"It's okay. I'll forget to take my sandwich if I'm not careful."

Tanya smiled at him again - she seemed to do that a lot - and busied herself making Gray's lunch.

"Do you remember everything your customers eat?" Gray couldn't hide the surprise in his voice.

"Yes," she said. "I have a good memory."

"Ah." Gray chided himself for thinking anyone would show an interest in him.

"Right, I'll make that flat white now."

"Yes, thanks."

She shifted her attention to the huge machine that hissed and spat like a chained beast.

"I've never asked. What is it you do?" She bashed depleted grounds out into the bin.

"Nothing interesting."

Tanya poured fresh coffee into the holder and tamped it down. "How uninteresting? And does it include a uniform?" She winked.

"It used to," admitted Gray. Back when he wasn't in CID.

A plume of steam hissed from the machine as Tanya wiggled levers and twisted knobs in a permutation which frankly mystified him. The noise meant no further conversation, so he waited patiently until she'd finished. She poured the steaming brown liquid into a large white ceramic cup on an equally large, misshapen saucer. She placed both on a tray next to a jug of frothy milk.

"Well, you don't look like a traffic warden or a security guard."

"That's because I'm not."

"So? Tell all!"

"I'm a policeman."

"That's nice." She placed his sandwich alongside the coffee. "I'll fetch your food over in a minute."

"Okay, thanks."

She flicked a strand of stray hair, tucked it behind an ear. Her eyes drifted to his left. Gray sensed the arrival of a new customer.

Gray headed over to his colleagues. All were quiet, scrutinising him.

"That looked cosy," said Fowler.

Hamson let out a laugh that caused a couple of people to turn and stare.

"We talked about the weather," said Gray, unable to think of anything better on the spur of the moment. He placed his tray on the table and took a seat.

"You protest too much, Sol," observed Carslake.

Thankfully his colleagues' meals arrived right then, breaking the commentary. Carslake leaned over and grabbed the pepper pot.

Gray kept quiet, allowing the others to quiz Pennance on his background, most of which he fended off. It was like watching a boxer on the defensive, gloves up, absorbing the blows which came at him from both left and right. There would be plenty of time for his own questions later, ones he didn't want to voice before the DCI.

As Tanya was bringing over Gray's eggs his mobile rang. "Excuse me." He moved away from the table. Carslake threw a questioning look his way. Gray ignored it.

"Good morning, DS Gray," the dour voice of the pathologist, Clough, sounding as lively as one of his cadavers.

"Hello, Ben." Gray often struggled to make a connection with people these days, but he and Clough were on the same page. "What can I do for you?"

"The suicide, Buckingham. I have his remains scheduled for the block today. I was enquiring whether you'd like to be present."

"Of course."

Clough sounded gratified. He rarely received visitors. He told Gray he had an hour before the procedure began.

"And there are one or two surprises, you might be pleased to hear," said Clough.

"Such as?"

"You'll have to wait. Otherwise where would be the fun?"

"And I have a surprise for you. A colleague will be joining us."

"Who?"

"You'll have to wait and see."

By the time Gray disconnected he didn't fancy either the eggs or coffee with the prospect of a messy post-mortem anyway. His stomach would be better off empty.

"Anything important?" said Carslake, picking his teeth with a thick fingernail.

"Just Clough. Buckingham's procedure is in an hour."

"So you had a word with the good doctor then?"

"Something like that, sir." It was only now that Gray remembered Carslake had told him to press Clough. "I assume you'd like to be present, DI Pennance?"

"Absolutely. Wouldn't miss it for anything."

"There's lots of reasons I could think of," said Fowler.

Carslake checked his watch. "Right, we'd better be off."

"DI Pennance and I will go straight to the post-mortem, sir," said Gray.

"Makes sense," said Carslake. "Gives you the chance to finish your breakfast."

At the signal to leave the others stood with a scraping of chairs. The DCI put a hand out and stopped Pennance, who was in the process of reaching for his wallet. "Guests never pay."

"Thank you, sir."

"Consider it my treat. Sol here will get it." Carslake winked at Gray. "See you back at the office."

Pennance finished the last of his bacon sandwich.

"Are you done?" asked Gray. Pennance nodded.

Gray stepped up to the counter and handed over some notes to Tanya, received a very small amount of change in return and a receipt he would doubtless forget to claim.

"See you tomorrow," he said.

The bell rattled as he left the café. Gray turned right and began the walk back to work.

"Excuse me!" Gray turned at Tanya's shout. She was standing in doorway, waving. "You forgot something."

His face colouring, Gray retraced his steps, leaving Pennance standing. Tanya held his sandwich bag up. He took it. "You left it on the table,"

"Told you I would. Sorry."

"I'm the one who should apologise."

"Why?"

"I realised after we spoke, you come here quite a lot and I'm supposed to have a good memory, yet I don't even know your name." Tanya looked at the ground.

"It's Sol."

"I'm Tanya," she said and held out her hand. Gray shook it. The warm little feeling in the pit of his stomach rekindled at a woman's touch.

Twenty

B en Clough eyed DI Pennance the way he'd regard a fungal infection on the sole of his foot. He turned to Gray and said, "I assume *this* is my surprise?"

"I hope I'm not too much of a disappointment," said Pennance and introduced himself. He made to shake hands. The pathologist held back, displaying his nitrile gloves.

"I'd reciprocate, but that would mean scrubbing up again."

"Next time, perhaps."

"There's always a next time, unfortunately."

"Quite."

"I'll crack on, then." Clough shouldered his way through a double swing door into the examination room, all white tiles and stainless steel, dazzling spotlights, glittering surgical instruments, and gaping drains, everything designed for an easy clean.

The viewing area was plain in comparison, as if the lion's share of the budget had been reserved for the dead. The walls were washed in a cornflower blue; rows of uncomfortable chairs were fixed to the floor, all facing the same direction. It was like a McDonald's restaurant, just more meat on show.

The air was icy and stank of disinfectant. Gray kept his coat on and breathed through his mouth. Pennance did the same. Gray would see what the DI was really made of once the slicing began.

Clough ensured the overhead microphone was working before he commenced. His voice issued from a nearby speaker: "Are you ready?"

Gray shook his head, eliciting a rare grin from Clough. He would drone incessantly throughout, recording everything, no matter how inconsequential, his voice a monotone as he relayed his findings.

Post-mortems always seemed to take a lot longer than they should. Perhaps it was one of those occasions where time really did slow to a crawl. Joyous events were over in a flash, yet misery stretched for an eternity. The more complicated procedures took hours to complete, sometimes as much as half a day.

Gray glanced at Pennance. The DI seemed entirely unmoved by the unnatural turning inside out of a body by evisceration, the blood on Clough's hands and clothes, and the removal and assessment of organs.

Over the next thirty minutes Gray kept his eyes averted. The possibility that this was his son on the slab wouldn't leave him, making him want to run out of the room, to throw up.

Gray attempted to tune out Clough's monologue.

A tap on Gray's shoulder. "Interesting, don't you think?" asked Pennance.

"What, sorry? I was somewhere else."

"How high was the railing on the balcony?"

Gray thought back, raised a hand to the approximate height. "About that."

"Clough said there's discolouration of the skin apparent on the lower back. More on the arms."

Pennance shut up for the rest of the examination, leaned forward with an unnerving intensity.

At last the pathologist removed his gloves, discarding them in a bin before washing thoroughly. When he exited the examination room the smell of disinfectant swept along in his wake.

"Not the most remarkable case I've ever seen," he said.

"You mentioned bruising, Doctor," said Pennance.

"Just here." Clough tapped the side of his hand on his back, just above the hip.

"In a narrow line?"

"You mean like the width of a railing?" Pennance nodded. "About right, I'd say."

"And the arms?"

"On the biceps. Perhaps a strong grip applied. Very recently. I looked for any swelling of the brain, in case he'd been violently shaken. It was impossible to tell, given the impact."

"So Buckingham could have been walked off the balcony?"

"It's possible, although that's your job to determine, not mine. There's more, before you focus on that one point. Signs of a historic drug use, injection marks in a variety of veins and by no means fresh. I've taken hair samples and sent them off to the lab to be sure. He could have been ingesting narcotics in a different manner. I'll put everything in my report."

Clough was thorough. If he said there was nothing else abnormal that would be the case. No point in pressing; it just annoyed the man.

"If there's nothing more, I'll leave you two alone." This time Clough held out his hand for Pennance to shake. "Until we meet again." The pathologist made his exit.

"Back to the station then, I guess," said Gray.

"That would be good. It'll give me chance to read the case notes."

"There's not much to go on."

"All part of a bigger picture."

"Would you care to explain what that picture is?"

Gray's phone rang. He answered.

"Are you on your way back?" said Carslake.

"Yes, all done here."

"I need to see you. Get your first impressions, and all that."

"Problem?" said Pennance when Gray had rung off.

Gray nodded. "You. Carslake wants my feedback. In private."

"I'm not surprised. Let's talk in the car. There's some stuff you should be aware of before you meet the boss."

It took five minutes to get out of the hospital and reach Gray's vehicle. He saw a traffic warden heading their way, but he was safe. He'd paid for a ticket which still had half an hour on it. Showing your badge didn't work anymore and there were plenty of news outlets that hungered for the slightest hint of police abuses. He wasn't willing to give Scully the benefit.

"Come on then," said Gray when they were inside. "Spill."

"What about Carslake?"

"He can wait. I'll say there was traffic."

Pennance stared out of the windscreen for a moment, gathering his thoughts. "All of this stays between us, right?"

"Scout's honour."

Pennance eyed Gray warily. "I'm being serious."

"So am I, sir."

"It's Marcus."

"Let's stick to the formalities, sir."

"You have an interesting past."

"So?"

"Your loss defines you."

"I think about them all the time."

"I understand. I would too."

"Are you married? Do you have kids?" asked Gray. He'd never bothered to find out about Pennance's personal life.

"No and no."

"Then you couldn't possibly understand what it's like to lose one."

"I work with children all the time."

"It's not the same as your own flesh and blood. The world changes as soon as you've got one of your own."

Pennance nodded. "I can't argue with that."

Satisfied he'd made his point, Gray let the argument go and moved on to the next. "I'm getting questions about the mobile. How the hell do I explain it to Carslake?"

"Leave it to me. I just need to choose my moment."

"Make sure it happens."

"You have my word."

"So what's this investigation Buckingham was so integral to?"

"First, I should tell you something about him, what kind of kid he was. Okay?"

"Sure." This was what Gray wanted, desperately.

"According to his file, Nick was born in London. His mother was a prostitute. She couldn't cope with a baby so he was taken into care when he was just a few months old. After that he moved from home to home, pretty much in trouble from the moment he could walk. By the age of twelve, Nick was on the streets. His carers didn't report him missing. He was already drinking and doing drugs at that point."

"Tell me something I can't figure out for myself."

"Consider this all context. Nick was picked up within days of being out of care, fed with the promise of money, which meant he could get off the streets and out of the cold. Next thing he knew, he was in a big car being taken to a swanky hotel. He was made to shower, then he spent a few hours with a man before he was given some money and kicked out. This went on for months. The same car, the same pimp. Different places, different punters.

"Nick wasn't stupid. His clients clearly valued youth and novelty so he knew his appeal could only last so long. He tried to kick his habit, tried to save some cash and live a different life, but he couldn't do it. He was caught in a vicious circle.

"But Nick had an ace up his sleeve. He suspected he had valuable information – he thought he recognised some of the people he'd spent the night with. However, they were in positions of power and Nick didn't know who to trust. Then he got himself arrested in Green Park. I heard about him from the cop who picked him up."

"Yandell?"

"Yes. He's one of my eyes on the street."

"What about Dent? Is she one of yours too?"

"Let's just say Rosemary operates more on the fringes. Like you."

"So you met Buckingham and he just gave up all of his information?"

"Of course not. Nick had a mistrust of the police to start with, never mind what other ideas were in his head. He assumed his clients were well-connected people; they clearly had money. Rosemary, over time, drew little snippets out of him. I only met Nick once there was some mutual trust built up. But then word got out that I was building a case against the wrong people."

"A mole inside the Met?"

Pennance nodded. "Those connections again. The city wasn't safe for Nick, so I called you. Sent him down here to get him out of harm's way."

"That didn't work."

"I appreciate your bluntness."

"It's a fortunate trait of mine. One thing I don't understand, though - if Nick was so valuable to you, why didn't he have an escort? A couple of friendly police to look after him?"

"I didn't know who was friendly, as you put it, and who wasn't. Some of the people I'm investigating are big and powerful, so yes, someone on the inside is certain."

"You don't believe Nick committed suicide?"

"No."

"Someone got to him?"

"On the basis of the bruises, it's possible."

"Who?"

"Now that's the big question. The problem is Nick wasn't supposed to be in that flat. I had another location for him to stay. He never turned up."

"So he went off the radar?"

"Apparently so."

"Why there?"

"I wish I knew. I'm not even sure it matters."

Gray was about to ask another question when his mobile rang. He answered and spoke before Carslake could. "Sorry, the traffic's crap. I'll be with you as soon as I can." He disconnected. "We'll have to continue this while we drive." Gray started the engine.

"That's about all I can tell you. For the time being, anyway."

"Who were his clients?"

"I can't tell you that."

"Then you do know more."

"I understand the point you're making but I'm not your enemy, Sol."

"You're clearly not my friend either. What else is going on?"

"I've already said too much."

Twenty One

Gray sloped into his boss's office.

"Sit down. I'll be with you in a minute." Carslake tapped away at his keyboard, using one digit per hand. Gray's own technique was equally laborious.

As Gray settled into his seat, there was a knock and Sylvia poked her head around the door. Sylvia altered her appearance regularly. Today was curls and arched eyebrows, although the glare meant for him remained consistent.

"Can I get you anything, DS Gray?" she said with everything other than enthusiasm.

"A whisky, if there's one going?"

"Very funny."

"It'll have to be a coffee then."

"As you wish." So much derision loaded into those three little words.

A worryingly short time later Sylvia re-entered without knocking this time, a chipped mug in one manicured claw. There was a distinct absence of steam.

"There you are." She smiled, dumped the mug on the desk and departed.

The contents were brown and sludgy. Like thick riverbank mud. Gray took a cautious sip, pulled a face, and set the offensive fluid back down again. Lukewarm, dirty engine oil was the best that could be said about it. Yesterday's reheated, in all probability.

Eventually, Carslake pushed the keyboard away and eyed Gray. "You took your bloody time getting here."

"Couldn't help it. Traffic. And since I've been hanging around for ten minutes I can't be that important."

"Superintendent trumps sergeant. How's the coffee?"

"Ancient."

"Like us," said Carslake as he settled into the chair adjacent to Gray.

Bugger. It's that kind of conversation. A face-to-face thing.

"How's everything with the team?"

This obviously wasn't what Carslake really wanted to discuss.

"All good, thanks. No issues to speak of."

"What about your appointment with Mallory?"

"Done."

"Excellent."

"That's it? Can I go?"

"No."

"There's a surprise?"

"Enough of the sarcasm." Carslake stood, moved towards the wall and leaned against it as if he needed support. He stared out of the window for a moment. Outside, a gull wheeled in the bluster. "How was the Buckingham post-mortem?"

"The usual. Depressing. I don't know how Clough does it, to be honest. Bottom line is it might not be a suicide after all."

"Why?"

Gray told him about the bruising on Nick Buckingham's back and arms.

"So he could have been pushed?"

"I'll have to make measurements to be sure, but possibly."

"And Pennance, what's he like?"

"Cool, efficient, focused on the job. Though I'm not sure I'd ever like him."

"Really? He seemed personable enough to me. Anyway, I've reassigned the Buckingham case to you. Before you ask, I told Hamson earlier and no, she wasn't happy about it. You and Pennance can handle it. I want him busy. I don't think he's here for what he says he is."

"You're not making sense."

"Think about it. Why would a DI come down all the way from London for some kid?"

Gray gritted his teeth, counted to ten. The kid who could have been Tom. "It looks like murder now. Isn't that enough?"

Carslake returned to his seat, leaned on his elbows. "But how could he have known? It doesn't hang together and I'm bloody worried he's playing me."

"I'd wondered the same thing."

"And your number on Buckingham's phone. How did that happen?"

Gray took in a sharp breath. He'd almost managed to forget about that. He tried to keep his voice steady: "Beats me."

"It needs dealing with," said Carslake. Gray couldn't agree more. "Down to Pennance, do you think?"

"If it is, he hasn't said so," lied Gray.

"I don't like it." Carslake rocked the chair back, a risky venture, given its age and the mass of the occupant. "The Met. Sapphire. Something bigger is going on."

"Like what?" Gray couldn't see what Carslake was getting at, but sometimes there was no arguing with him.

"I've no idea and that's precisely why I'm unhappy. So you need to do something about it."

"Me? What the hell can I do?"

"You can be my eyes and ears on this thing. Keep me informed of what Pennance is up to. You're down in the office all the time. I'm up here."

If Gray wanted to tell Carslake about Pennance, now was the time. But he held his tongue for too long and Carslake moved on.

"I appreciate this, Sol."

GRAY STEPPED BACK INTO the CID office. Fowler glanced up from a report he was typing.

"Looks like your blood pressure's up, Sol. Wouldn't want you dying on us. Couldn't stand all the administration."

The DS laughed at his own joke and Gray forced himself to join in. He moved away from Fowler and crossed to Hamson's desk.

"Where's Pennance?" said Gray.

"He's appropriated one of the meeting rooms as an office. What's up?"

"Pennance, followed by Carslake. It's enough to drive you to drink."

A snort from Hamson said she felt the same. Gray's desk phone interrupted. It was the desk sergeant.

"Got a visitor for you."

"Who?"

"She won't say."

"I'll be there in a minute." Gray told Hamson where he was going – to the front desk, then out. "Over to the jetty, I could do with some fresh air and clear my head. I'll have my mobile if anyone needs me."

"Sol, I almost forgot to tell you ..." said Fowler.

Gray muttered an expletive, said, "Quickly."

"Don't bother yourself then. It's only about Buckingham. I guess a murdered kid doesn't matter."

"I'm not in the best of moods."

"That's not my fault."

Which was true. Gray ground out an apology which Fowler seemed to grudgingly accept.

"Buckingham wasn't signing on," said Fowler. "There aren't records of him and nobody at the dole office recognised his picture."

That was unusual. Gray had expected benefits to be Buckingham's top priority. "And the flat?"

"The owner is a Patrick Silverman. He bought it when the place was built back in 1963."

"And where's Silverman now?"

"Passed away four years ago in an old people's home where he'd lived since the late '90s."

It didn't make sense. Gray frowned. "No will? No next of kin?"

"Neither. It looks like the council had no idea he was dead. All the bills were still being paid."

"By who?"

Fowler shrugged. "I hadn't got that far."

A thought struck Gray. He rapped his fingers twice on Fowler's desk. "Give the home a call, would you? See what they say about Silverman and his funds."

"Sure thing. I hear the case is all yours."

"Carslake gave me a day's grace. This will be the last request."

"You'll owe me a beer."

"Done."

When Gray reached the front desk, Morgan wasn't there. And neither was his nameless visitor.

Twenty Two

Bloody Carslake's politics, bloody Pennance's secrecy, and bloody selfish behaviour threatened everything. And Gray was stuck in the middle. His head felt ready to burst from the pressure.

He scooted across Fort Hill, dodging traffic. Past the art gallery. Within ten minutes he was outside Tanya's café. He pulled at the door, but it didn't budge. Gray peered through the glass. The lights were on, but it was empty. When he stepped back he noticed a handwritten sign on the door which said, "Back soon."

Gray partially retraced his steps. He turned left before the gallery, wandered out along the harbour arm which protected the moorings of a few bonny boats from the stormy English Channel, which stirred on the other side of the sturdy concrete and brick structure.

Near the end of the arm was a café which had set up in one of the squat, redundant fishing buildings. Once the day's catch would have been hauled here, gutted, processed and transported on.

He ducked inside and ordered a coffee. A search of his pockets came up empty. He apologised and departed. Face burning with embarrassment, Gray carried on until another step meant a twenty-foot drop into the sea. Here was a statue, a faceless lady constructed entirely of shells. She stared impassively outwards, standing tall whatever the elements threw at her.

The relative calm was soon interrupted by the ring of Gray's mobile. The display revealed it was Fowler. Hopefully earning that pint.

"Good news?"

"I spoke to Shady Oaks, the retirement home. Silverman's payments went through an intermediary."

"What does that mean?"

"Everything was handled by a legal firm."

"Sounds expensive."

"I wouldn't know. It's Neil Wright and Partners."

"Which means Frank McGavin," said Gray.

"Yes."

"Now I'm even gladder the case is yours," said Fowler and disconnected.

Wright was well-known to Gray and his colleagues. A crooked notary who worked exclusively for criminals, the most notable of whom was Frank McGavin, who ran everything illegal in Thanet.

Wright was smoother than margarine. No one in the force's history had managed to raise a charge against him, never mind present it. The same went for McGavin. Whenever McGavin's name came up in an investigation it meant no good, but making a charge stick was the challenge. Wright looked after McGavin and vice versa.

Gray considered what he knew, which wasn't very much.

A suicide, or possible murder victim, who'd once been on the game, but no more, living in a flat owned by a man long dead, which was managed by a firm of criminal defence lawyers.

And then there was the Pennance conundrum. Were Carslake's suspicions correct? Was the DI here for something completely unrelated?

And the events before Buckingham's death. Yes, there had been a suicide note – had it been a cry for help? And the bruising? The unidentified fingerprints on the glass? Whose were they?

Gray knew very little of relevance. However, thanks to Fowler, he at least had a thread to pull on. Mr Wright would be getting a visit.

Gray pulled the photo of Buckingham out of his pocket. It was beginning to crease. He stared into the boy's face.

A voice interrupted him. "Penny for them."

Tanya was standing to the right of the shell lady, like a child next to its mother, such was the difference in height. Gray slid the photo away. Tanya proffered a cardboard cup. He accepted, felt heat, and not just from the drink.

"I called in to see you," said Tanya. "They said you were over here."

"Thanks." He took a sip. Decent coffee. One of Tanya's own. "This is a surprise."

"A pleasant one, I hope? Because I don't think my fragile self-confidence could take it otherwise."

"Of course. I just didn't expect to see you."

"Why not?"

"It's not the sort of thing that usually happens to me."

"Thing?"

"You know. A beautiful woman, looking for me."

"I must be fatally flawed, then."

"Maybe."

"I love this spot."

"Me too. It's where I come to think. When the office gets too loud."

"Do you want me to go?"

"No."

"Cheers." Tanya held out her cup to Gray. He nudged his into hers.

"Cheers," he said.

"So tell me about yourself."

"What do you want to know?"

"More than I do now."

"Which is?"

"You're a cop. You're stressed. You live alone."

"I might be married."

"You're not."

"Is it that obvious?"

"I'm divorced too. We survivors of the broken ring can always tell."

"We never divorced." He paused. "She died."

"Oh. I'm sorry." Tanya held a hand up to her mouth, her eyes wide.

"It was a long time ago."

"God, I wish I'd never opened my mouth."

"How were you to know?"

"Even so..."

"Forget about it. What about you? I don't hear a local accent."

"Met a boy, got pregnant too young, moved here because of husband's job, husband runs off with secretary, single mother raises children, then they bugger off too."

"Sounds like life's been hard."

"Not really. I was better off without him. The kids have turned out well and I've got a job I love. There's only one thing I'm missing."

"What's that?"

Before Tanya could answer, Gray's phone rang. "Bloody hell, the bloody thing never shuts up."

"Answer it."

"Solomon, thank God. Thank God. Thank God it's you!" Gray recognised the panicked voice immediately. Alice Newbold from St Peter's Church. "Something terrible's happened, Solomon."

"What is it? What's the matter, Alice?"

"It's David. He's dead."

Twenty Three

Fowler drove while Gray made the call to Forensics. A minute after receiving Alice's call Fowler had picked Gray up from outside the gallery. Gray was still breathless after the headlong dash.

"SOCO are moving," said Gray.

Hamson nodded from the passenger seat.

Gray spent the rest of the journey hanging on for dear life as Fowler threw the patrol car around corners, lights flashing and sirens blaring. Ten heart-stopping minutes later Fowler jerked to a halt on the High Street in front of the church. A few commuters stopped to stare at the noise of rubber on tarmac. Fowler appeared to have enjoyed the experience. Gray couldn't say the same. It was all he could do not to throw up.

Gray led the way into the church. He noticed the decorations were finished. Simple sprays and wreaths of holly and ivy, one at the end of each pew. A Christmas tree, the lights switched off, was standing near the pulpit. Alice occupied a pew at the very front, the same space she'd had for as long as Gray could remember, closest to the word of God that issued from successive vicars' mouths. She was staring with reddened eyes at the stained-glass windows, her hands clasped, mumbling prayers beneath her breath. Maybe seeing the nailed deity, maybe not.

"Alice?" Gray placed a gentle hand on the old woman's shoulder. Her face was as pallid as one of the statues who guarded the dead outside.

"We'll give you a moment," said Hamson in a low voice. She and Fowler moved off. Gray was keen to follow, but Alice demanded his attention.

"How are you?" he asked.

"That's a bit touchy-feely for a policeman, isn't it?" She attempted a smile, but couldn't quite pull it off.

"You know me."

"Which is why I asked. I'm trying hard not to be sick."

"An entirely normal reaction. I'd be worried if you were full of the joys of Christmas."

"Well you can rest assured that I'm feeling anything but festive." Alice exhaled heavily. "None of this makes any sense. Why would somebody kill David?"

"I've no idea. That's what I'm here to find out. When did you last see him alive?"

"Yesterday evening. I stayed behind as usual to tidy up after evensong."

"How did he seem?"

"The same as always. Better, in fact. Full of energy for the challenges ahead."

"What challenges?"

"The usual. Raising money for the tower repairs, growing the congregation. And a new task, one that really had him going."

"Which was?"

"You, Solomon."

"What?"

"You were his newest trial." Alice nodded to emphasise the point. "He was down after you left the other day, but within twenty-four hours he was back up again, bouncing around like a jackrabbit. He was sure you were here for a reason."

"I was sheltering from the rain."

"It was more than that. He believed God was calling you home."

"I don't believe in God anymore, Alice."

"Kate was my best friend. I miss her too. The Lord tests us all, repeatedly. But we should never stop believing."

"I did. A long time before Kate left this world."

Alice nodded. "But David never doubted your faith. For him you coming here that day was a sign."

"So why is he dead? Is that a sign too?"

As soon as the words were out of his mouth Gray knew he shouldn't have uttered them. Alice's face drooped. The colour that had appeared in her cheeks as a result of their discussion melted away. She shifted her eyes forward again.

"I told him you were beyond redemption, that you were Godless, and that he was wasting his time."

"I'm sorry."

"So am I. Please, why don't you join your colleagues? Leave me with my Lord. I'm not going anywhere."

"Sure. Where is...?"

"David is by the altar."

Gray found Fowler and Hamson outside standing on a grass strip opposite the church door. Behind them were a couple of rows of the oldest grave markers, then a high stone wall. Fowler was rolling a cigarette. Hamson had installed uniforms at the main front gate and side entrance from the supermarket. A tape cordon was already strung out as a demarcation.

Gray motioned Hamson over. He stood in the church doorway, half an eye on Alice. He put a finger up to his lips to indicate quiet was needed.

"Any luck with the witness?" asked Hamson, speaking softly.

"Alice says she found him earlier. She hadn't seen him since last night."

"We'll get a rough time of death from Clough in a bit. Anything else?"

"Not really. I need you to do me a favour, Von." Hamson rolled her eyes. "Can you speak with Alice, see if there's anything else she knows?"

"What's the problem? I thought you knew her."

"We managed to drift into a theological argument. She tried to bring me back into the fold."

"You basically told her God didn't exist, didn't you?"

"That was the gist of it, yes. Apparently I'm beyond redemption."

Hamson huffed. "Leave it to me."

Gray crossed the path to Fowler who was now sucking on his cigarette. "Have you told your wife about all this yet?"

"I thought I'd leave that to Alice."

"She'll be beside herself when she finds out."

"I know. That's why someone else can deal with it."

WHEN FORENSICS ARRIVED, Fowler was on his third cigarette in a row. He and Gray had maintained a stilted silence during the intervening period, Fowler preferring to tap away on his mobile rather than interact. Which was fine with Gray.

Brian Blake and his men bundled out of their vans and delivered a brief apology about being "tied up." Fowler smirked. Ben Clough arrived moments later, preventing Fowler from offering up a joke.

Until now the police presence had been unobtrusive. With the arrival of several bloody great white vehicles with *Forensic Team* stamped all over the side, that all changed.

Gray brought the Crime Scene Manager and pathologist up to date with the situation. The officious Blake stalked off to deal with the mundane administration. Only then could Clough access the church and finally make real progress.

Blake returned moments later. "There's an old woman inside," he said, huffy and unimpressed.

"Alice Newbold. She found the body," said Gray. "And Hamson's with her. She seems to be suffering a bit of shock."

"That's not the point. It's a crime scene."

"Just leave it, Blake. Have a heart."

Blake looked set to argue, even opened his mouth to do so, but caught sight of Hamson emerging from the church. He reconsidered, nodded at Clough to proceed, and took his leave without another word.

"Well?" Gray asked as Hamson walked towards him.

"I didn't get any more out of her than you did," said Hamson. "She seemed in a kind of fugue state. She won't budge. Whatever you said to her apparently shut her down."

Twenty Four

Five Years Ago
   "You need to come home," Alice told Gray on the phone, her voice laced with urgency. "Now."

"Why?"

"It's Kate."

Gray asked what had happened, but Alice was already gone. He rang back immediately to discover she'd left the phone off the hook, the line now engaged.

He drove like a man with the hounds of Hell snapping at his heels, cutting through the mid-morning traffic with abandon. Alice's call had been as urgent as it was unsettling. He needed to get home. Now. Not to where he now lived. To what had been theirs.

An ambulance, both doors wide open, stood at the kerb. Activity was unhurried, which meant they had no one to save.

The front door to the property yawned open. It was dark in the hall, despite the brightness of the sun. Gray went inside, his sense of dread growing with every new possible discovery. He could not explain why, but he felt drawn upstairs, one creaking step at a time.

Alice appeared in the entrance to the master bedroom. Somehow her face had lost its structure, as if her bones had melted and the flesh followed suit.

"I'm so sorry," she said, stepping aside, lifting her hands to her heart.

Gray entered with the eyes of a cop. Husband and father, guilt and grief roles forgotten for now.

Upstairs it was lighter, the curtains open. His wife lay in bed, propped up by pillows. She looked asleep, Bible in one hand. A photograph of Tom, the frame pointed towards Kate.

Margaret Fowler perched in a chair next to her friend, corpse-like herself. She took no notice of Gray; had eyes only for the dead.

Alice took Gray's silence for an inability to ask the question, so she filled in the gap: "I came round because we had plans. When she didn't answer, I let myself in. I found her like this and dialled 999. The paramedics think she took pills. A lot of them."

"You have keys?" asked Gray.

Alice nodded. "Of course. Margaret does too."

"Did you touch anything?" asked Gray.

"I checked her pulse and closed her eyelids when it was obvious she was in the hands of God. That was all."

"Where's Hope? Does she know?"

"No. You should be the one who tells her."

Nothing could be done for Kate. Drowning in the all-too-familiar numbness of shock, Gray forced himself to focus on what was left of his family. He spun on his heel, descended the stairs. He walked the half-mile to Hope's school, Dane Court. Gray wondered what he was going to tell her.

First her brother, now her mother...

Twenty Five

Clough emerged from the church and crooked a finger before ducking back inside. Suitably garbed in forensic suits and overshoes, Gray, Hamson, and Fowler finally had the chance to view the corpse.

Reverend Hill lay sprawled at the very front of the church, in the chancel before the altar, an area reserved for the clergy. The first sign of death was the blood. It had spread across the stone floor like a gory lagoon. Gray never ceased to be amazed by how much mess ten pints could make.

In order to access the body without contaminating the scene, metal plates had been placed on the floor which acted like stepping stones. Clough beckoned the trio over.

"He was shot twice. Head and back," he said.

"Which first?"

"I would guess head, took half his face off. There's a mark in the wall over there." Clough pointed. Low down, Gray saw a patch of light stone against dark where a chunk of the brickwork had been taken out. "Then the *coup de grâce* when prostrate."

"Why the second bullet?" asked Gray. "It's excessive. He'd have been dead before he hit the floor."

"Panic?" said Hamson. "One more just to make sure?"

Gray shook his head. "Possibly. Could be the shooter was angry with Hill over something."

"Time of death?" asked Hamson.

Clough pursed his lips. The question he was always asked, and the one Gray knew was the hardest to answer. Time of death estimates were often problematic. The calculation was based on three key aspects: the process of rigor mortis, the cooling of the body, and the settling of blood which started the moment the heart stopped.

All three were affected by airflow, temperature and moisture, and each locale varied. Clough repeated his little speech every time a detective asked the inevitable, and he did so again, pointing out the heat-conducting effects of the stone floor and the convection via the draughty windows.

"What would be your best guess, Doctor?"

"Some time in the last twelve hours."

"Roughly fits with the timescale outlined by Alice," said Gray. "May we?"

"Be my guest," said Clough, stepping aside. Fowler hung back while Gray and Hamson regarded the corpse in silence for a few moments. There was a wooden cross affixed to the wall. Jesus stared down at them from his position of torture.

"I'd guess he was kneeling here. Praying," said Gray eventually. His skull shattered by the bullet, limbs unable to break his fall. "The killer was a few paces behind the victim. Close enough not to miss."

Hamson nodded. "Went down like a sack of spuds."

"What about the shots themselves? Someone must have heard them?" asked Hamson.

"Not necessarily. The walls are thick and the church is set back from the road."

Gray had stood outside several times while a service was being held and nothing had reached his ears.

"David called me recently, wanting my help," said Gray.

"Do you think it's related?"

"No idea."

"I don't think there's much more to see here," said Hamson. Gray agreed. "He's all yours, Doctor."

Fowler had disappeared somewhere. Probably for a smoke. They found Blake conferring with one of his colleagues and asked him about the bullets

"We've got one so far. The other I expect to find when we move the corpse." Blake passed over a vial which contained a mangled chunk of metal at the bottom.

"Hopefully Ballistics can get something from that," said Hamson.

Gray examined it briefly. "I wouldn't bet on it. It's mashed into a pulp."

"Casings?"

Blake shook his head.

"Could be a revolver. They'd be retained within the chamber," said Gray.

"Or the killer was calm enough to pick them up." said Hamson.

"Maybe," said Blake.

"Cold."

"Calculating."

"A woman, then," predicted Blake.

"Sexist bastard."

"Just experienced."

Gray dragged Hamson away before she slapped Blake senseless.

GRAY STEPPED ASIDE, allowing Hamson to enter the vicarage ahead of him. Even though his fingers were encased in nitrile gloves, Gray tried not to touch anything.

Retracing his steps of only a few days ago, Gray entered the living room. It was pretty much the same as before, though Alice had cleared away the tea paraphernalia.

Gray pointed Hamson towards the kitchen and re-entered the small hallway himself. Beyond was the front door, to his right a further reception room which doubled as an office. He twisted the handle, went inside. The room was dark, the curtains tightly drawn. He flicked on the light.

Not much to see. A desk, chair, filing cabinet, and some shelves. On the desk was a paperwork tray. Gray leaned over and drew back the curtains. They'd been obscuring an Internet router. It was on, a single green light shining. Which meant a computer or laptop somewhere.

He pulled the chair away from the desk and bent down. There was the monitor and keyboard, propped up at the back of the footwell along with an inkjet printer. He moved them to one side, saw loose wires that would connect the desktop to the peripherals. But no computer.

Gray headed back to the church. Alice was no longer there. Blake must have insisted she be moved. He eventually found her in the back of a police car parked on the street. Margaret Fowler sat beside her. Both had bowed heads, lips moving in sync. They held hands.

As Gray neared them, Alice lifted her gaze to meet his. Her expression was stoic and she scrutinised every step Gray took. He opened the door, squatted.

"I have a question," he said. Alice just glared. "The computer in the Reverend's office - where is it?"

"It broke, so he sent it away for repair."

"To who?"

"I have no idea. David dealt with that kind of thing."

Alice turned away from him and closed her eyes again.

He wondered where the computer was and whether its absence was significant. He didn't have an answer, but perhaps God did.

Not that he'd be asking...

Twenty Six

The Incident Room shifted from a place of relative peace to one of bustle at the flick of a switch. CID bodies filled the space. Fowler began writing the case up onto the white-board. When he moved to rub the Buckingham details away, Gray stopped him. "There's enough space. Leave it up for now."

"A vicar shot to death in his own church. The press are going to be all over this one," said Hamson.

"Mercifully that's not something I'll have to deal with," said Gray. "You and Carslake can take that one."

"Thanks."

"Don't mention it."

Hamson clapped her hands in an effort to bring order. "Right, enough now, you lot!" The tangle of figures ordered themselves at the DI's call to arms. Faces switched front, discussions and speculation suspended.

"For those of you who aren't already aware, a local vicar by the name of David Hill was murdered sometime yesterday afternoon. Hill was last seen alive at ten o'clock yesterday evening. Gunshot wounds to the back of the head and torso fired at close range, we assume while he was praying. Neither the murder weapon nor the casings have been recovered. Two badly damaged bullets are on their way to Ballistics as we speak..."

The door opened, stopping Hamson mid-sentence. All heads turned to the interloper, Pennance, cup of coffee in hand and a surprised look on his face. He paused in the entrance, said, "Apologies for interrupting." Slightly red in the face, he gently closed the door, sidled around the circumference until he reached Gray.

"What's going on?" he whispered.

Gray gave him a brief summary, half an ear on Hamson who'd resumed her rundown of events. "There's just no respect for the church anymore," Pennance said.

"Any reason why there would be? Given the news over recent years, it's hardly surprising."

"You're biased."

Gray shrugged. "I can live with that. We'll require the meeting room from now on, sir."

"The meeting room?"

"I believe you've turned it into a temporary office."

"Oh, no problem, I'll move to wherever's convenient."

Hamson wrapped up her brief assessment and began assigning roles to the team.

"Is there anything I can help with?" asked Pennance. "I'm not making much headway with Buckingham."

"Depends what you can offer," said Gray.

The DI wriggled his fingers. "I'm pretty good with technology."

A thought struck Gray. He explained to Pennance what he'd found in David Hill's study, or more precisely, what he hadn't.

"The arrangement looked pretty casual," explained Gray. "I'll get one of the DCs to check into it, phone all the repair places."

"Let me see what I can find."

"Thanks, but we'll be fine, there can't be that many."

"You're a dinosaur, Sol. I can achieve a lot without actual access to the reverend's unit. Check into his online presence, see if he had any cloud-based files, social media accounts."

"Social media?"

"Yes, like Facebook or Twitter."

"I know what social media is. I'm just surprised the church would need access to something like that."

"It's the way the world communicates, Sergeant. God is no different."

"Fair enough. There might be something else as well. It's probably irrelevant."

"All data is relevant at this stage, you know that."

"David kept calling me about something. He called it 'the devil's work.'"

"What did he mean?"

"No idea. He wanted me to go over and help him."

"Did you?"

"I didn't get the chance."

"All right. I'll find out who his ISP is and check out what websites he was visiting."

"In that case, you're hired. I'll tell Hamson."

"Point me towards a workstation."

"Use my desk. I've something else to do." He wouldn't bother telling Pennance or the boss what he was up to. Not yet anyway.

Twenty Seven

Pennance was on Gray's mind the entire trip to Canterbury. Gray was stabbing at the button to make the doors open as the train slowed. The doors refused to open until the train had completely stopped. Their stubbornness did little to help Gray's mood. He stepped out of the carriage and shoved his way through a crowd of people waiting to take his place.

A cool breeze cut through Gray's jacket. He walked faster to warm himself. Within minutes he was at the West Gate. A brick wall once surrounded the entire city, constructed by the Romans and reinforced at the end of the fourteenth century when fears of a French invasion were at their height.

The offensive never materialised and as the need for accommodation expanded, the walls, and then the gates fell as a result of social change rather than war. The West Gate was the last of twenty-four, standing in defiance against time and progress.

Within the walls was a pedestrianised road which still followed the route laid down by the Romans, probably overlaying the original Iron Age track. Gray knew all this because he had been a bit of a history buff until the past became somewhere he no longer wished to visit.

Canterbury reminded Gray of a cross between Cambridge and York, full of chic boutiques, eateries, and smaller chain stores. It was a consumer's heaven. He hated the place.

As a result of his dislike it had been a while since he'd last been to the city, dominated by its huge cathedral. Gray took a detour down a side road a couple of hundred yards beyond the West Gate, away from the main thoroughfare and its crowds. There he passed the grand cathedral entrance, a magnificence of carvings and statues in grey stone, swapping shoppers and casual coffee consumers for tourists.

Outside there was the usual gaggle of tourists taking photos and debating whether to stump up the hefty admission fee to the guard in his box. The cathedral was one of those sites where the public could only gain entry by paying, despite having provided the funds to build it in the first place. Another dichotomy of organised religion.

When a Chinese tourist approached asking whether he could take a poignant image of the visitors for posterity, Gray moved off, shaking his head.

Neil Wright and Partners was located at the opposite side of the central thoroughfare, so Gray cut up another side road and weaved through the flow of pedestrians once more. This next street was relatively quiet, despite the hubbub just yards away. Wright's office was halfway along, on the second floor of the building he now faced.

Gray entered and climbed the stairs. No formal reception here. Relatively low-cost rentals. He found himself in a corridor with closed doors left and right. Each had a plaque outside identifying the business. Gray hit upon the right one and went in unannounced.

"GOOD AFTERNOON, SERGEANT," said Wright. Neither his tone nor demeanour betrayed any surprise at Gray's arrival. Sharp eyes absorbed the DS at a glance. Wright was suitably distinguished in a smart shirt open at the neck to reveal a rich tan which Gray suspected was cultivated on a beach somewhere hot and exclusive, rather than a sunbed or spray booth. Gray felt rather shabby in comparison. "Are you here to engage me in some work?"

"As if I would."

"You'd be surprised, Solomon."

"It's DS Gray."

"Of course."

Wright smiled like he'd seen it all before, as if Gray was someone collecting for a charity. A few pennies to get rid of a minor irritation. Or a thick wedge of notes in a brown envelope.

Because that was Wright's business, taking care of problems his criminal clients couldn't. He was the sole occupant of these small offices. No employees, which presumably reduced potential trust issues. Wright didn't advertise, didn't take walk-in business. He didn't need to.

Gray had no idea who the Partners in the company name were. Maybe they were an affectation, or they'd been dispensed with long ago. Maybe they'd never existed in the first place. He didn't care.

Wright waved at the visitor's chair, grander than his own modest affair, doubtless designed to put his clients, rather than himself, on a pedestal. So much the opposite of Carslake. Gray declined. His mobile rang. He ignored the vibration in his pocket.

"I'm just a—" Wright started.

"Businessman," Gray interrupted. "I know. I've heard it all before."

Wright smiled once more, and this time it appeared almost genuine. He leaned back in his seat, spread his arms in a welcoming pose. "So, are you going to tell me what this is about?"

"Patrick Silverman."

Wright affected a blank stare. "That's all I get?"

"He was one of your clients."

"If you say so. I have lots of clients. I can't be expected to remember them all."

"I'll jog your memory. He's not your usual type."

"What is my 'usual', Sergeant?"

"Crooks."

Wright burst out laughing, slapped the desk with an open palm. "I like it, but that's slander, DS Gray, and I happen to know a perfectly good lawyer who could prove that point in court."

"It's fact."

The solicitor shrugged. "Depends on how you define crooks. There have been plenty of examples in the press recently of people with a pristine public image who had more blood on their hands and destroyed more lives than the worst serial killers."

Gray agreed, though wasn't about to let Wright know it. "Patrick Silverman resided in the Shady Oaks residential home in Herne Bay."

"You make it sound like he no longer does."

"Correct. He passed away."

"Passed away? So quaint."

"Hardly, Mr Wright. I've seen death and its consequences too many times."

"My heart bleeds."

"And here I was thinking your heart was in a jar of formaldehyde somewhere."

Wright pursed his lips. "I'm a very busy man, Sergeant. So unless you happen to have a warrant, I'd like you to leave."

"Fine by me. I don't want to be here any longer than necessary. One last thing, though. Silverman owns a flat in Arlington House, Margate. Except he's been dead for four years. The bills for his care were and still are handled by your company."

Wright shrugged. "It's not that unusual. We probably have power of attorney. No one told us the old boy had died, so we carried on coughing up and the care home carried on taking the money, I would assume. You should be investigating them."

"Who would have paid you?"

"As I don't remember Silverman, I certainly wouldn't be able to recall the associated financial relationships."

"Hazard a guess. What's typical?"

"It could have been anyone. A relative, for example. A sibling who inherited and wanted the old boy out of the way."

"Does that happen often?"

"More than you'd think. At least it won't be a problem you'll face." Wright grinned.

Gray remained calm. "What about Frank McGavin? Would he be paying?"

"Who?"

"Don't pull that one. You and I know him all too well."

"That's a new one on me, Sergeant." Wright was inscrutable. He'd make a great card player.

"I have a hunch someone like Frank would be involved."

"First name terms. It sounds like you're more acquainted with him than I am."

"Only in a legal sense. And you haven't answered my question."

"I'd have to check my records."

"So check."

Wright relented and tapped away at his laptop. "I digitised all my data last summer."

"Very modern." Gray wished the police would do the same. Some information was electronic, some not. The older stuff was still on paper, gathering dust, being nibbled at by mice.

"Four years ago, you say?"

"Yes."

"Okay, let's see what comes up," said Wright, as he melodramatically slapped at a key and sat back in his chair. "And the response is... nothing. I don't have any record of a Patrick Silverman."

Gray strode around the desk, barging past Wright.

"You only needed to ask, Solomon."

The screen showed a search box with "Silverman, David" entered. The feedback below said "0 results." Gray deleted the name and retyped it. He struck the enter key. The computer barely paused in its consideration before spitting out an identical result. Gray raised a questioning eyebrow at Wright who raised a disinterested shoulder in return.

"It could be that the information simply wasn't transferred properly. We used a temp. Cheap, but she made mistakes."

"You've had this before?"

"A couple of times."

"Where are your physical records?"

"Shredded. They took up a significant amount of space and I didn't need them once everything was on here." Wright tapped the laptop.

"Not everything is, though."

"Sometimes that's life. Sorry, there's nothing else I can do." He didn't sound or look apologetic.

Gray had no legal recourse, no warrant, not even permission from his senior officer. It was stalemate, and both men knew it. Gray threw his card on the lawyer's desk. "In case you think of anything."

"Of course." Wright picked up the card and dropped it into the bin.

BACK IN MARGATE THE taxi pulled up in front of the station. It was pissing down. Gray paid, didn't tip, and went inside.

"DI Hamson has been looking for you," said Morgan the desk sergeant who was rarely away from his post. Morgan's mouth twitched with amusement, making his ratty moustache do the same.

"Lucky me."

"She said to go straight through when you're back."

"Did she now?"

"How was your date?" said Morgan, smirking.

"What date?"

"With the woman who came in to see you the other day."

Gray thought back. Tanya said she'd popped in only to find he'd gone out. "Good, thanks."

"You're a lucky man." The desk sergeant seemed to be on the verge of an amused outburst.

Wondering what he'd missed, Gray headed through to the offices. Hamson wasn't in the detective's office, although Pennance was, talking to Fowler, his back to the door. Gray's scowl caused Fowler to halt mid-flow. Pennance followed the man's gaze, twisted his neck and met Gray's stare. He returned his attention briefly to Fowler.

"Thanks, I appreciate the information. Let's finish our discussion later, okay?"

As Pennance made his way to Gray's desk, Fowler threw him an apologetic shrug.

"I was wondering where you'd got to," said Pennance.

"I didn't realise I was supposed to appraise you of my movements. I'm just about to visit the toilets. Is that something you'd like to be aware of, Inspector?"

"Not my sort of thing, to be honest."

"I'm glad we've cleared that up. It's late. Probably a sensible idea to get you back to the hotel."

"DI Hamson has offered to take me."

"Very helpful is our Yvonne, but I'll do it. Where's your bag, by the way?"

"I already checked in this morning. I'll just grab my coat."

"Don't rush. Hamson wants to see me first."

As soon as Pennance cleared out, Gray crossed to Fowler's desk. "What was he after?"

"Just wanted to know what I'd found out so far regarding Buckingham."

"Did you tell him about the lawyer?"

"You said not to mention Wright. So I didn't."

"Good."

Hamson was alone in the incident room, staring at the whiteboard. "Ah, the wanderer returns. Now where the hell have you been?"

"Checking out computer repair shops," Gray lied.

"We've got uniforms for that. I needed you here."

"You were busy. I just got on with it."

"I tried calling. Several times."

"Did you? Battery must be flat."

"What are you up to, Sol?"

"Me? Nothing." Gray tried to look innocent. "Anyway, Pennance wants a lie down. He asked me to give him a lift to the hotel."

"I was going to do that."

"Somebody must have warned him off."

Gray made a dash for the door, managed to get through it before Hamson had anything substantial to hand to fling at him.

"Ready?" said Pennance.

"I'd suggest you stick that on." Gray nodded to the raincoat over Pennance's arm. It looked barely up to the job, probably unable to cope with the temperature in his car, never mind the weather outside. "It's raw out."

In the car park Pennance pulled the fabric tightly about him to keep out the bitter wind. "You were right."

"It happens sometimes."

The return journey along the seafront took slightly longer than Gray's taxi journey from the station. They were briefly held up at the clock tower roundabout, where the council periodically changed the layout, regardless of the cost and confusion to the public. Past the bright lights of Dreamland, once a major tourist attraction and now a faded relic, like the town itself.

Dreamland was closed these days, the dodgems and rollercoaster silent, the merry-go-round mothballed. There was a hope to regenerate it in the near future. Plans had been drawn up and torn up more times than could be counted, although this time there was some luminary designer involved. Time would tell if celebrity stardust made the slightest difference.

Gray was lucky enough to nab a bay adjacent to the hotel entrance. It was one of those places with an identity crisis, doing cheap food, kids' parties, and overnight stays. All things to all people. There'd be plenty of Londoners down to see the art gallery's displays who'd regret booking in here with the local hoi polloi.

Gray locked up once Pennance had wriggled out. He felt eyes upon him and looked over to Buenos Ayres, a row of terraced houses near the hotel. A tramp stared at them. Big guy.

"Know him?" said Pennance.

"Of him, yes. Trouble. I'd advise you stay well clear."

Pennance held out his hand for Gray to shake. "I appreciate your help today."

"No problem." Gray wondered what "help" Pennance was referring to. "What time do you want me to pick you up in the morning?"

"I'll walk."

"See you tomorrow, then."

Pennance nodded.

Gray returned to his car. He sat there for a few minutes, trying to work out what Pennance really wanted. There was something about the man, like he had a higher purpose in life compared to the rest of the population. Gray gave up, figuring he'd find out at some point. That's what he always did, waited for the impending to reveal itself. He'd had a lot of practice.

Gray put the key into the ignition. Before he could start the engine his mobile rang.

He thought he'd better answer it, but immediately wished he hadn't.

"Hello Sergeant, Ed Scully here. How are you?"

"Just gone from bad to worse."

"I'll take that as a compliment."

"What do you want? I'm busy."

"So I understand. I was hoping for some copy from you before we go to print. Well, to be more accurate, before the article goes online. Print is so yesterday."

"What article?"

"About the murders. The ones you've been keeping quiet about."

Gray stifled a groan. This was all he needed. He was damned if he was going to give anything to Scully. Over his dead body. Or the reporter's. "No idea what you're talking about."

Scully laughed, a slippery, wet sound. "I was rather hoping you'd say that. So I'll put down 'The officer running the investigation declined to respond'. Sounds suitably incompetent, don't you think?"

"Whatever. I stopped caring what you and your equally thick readers believed a long, long time ago."

"My readers love you, Sergeant. You're great copy. Always screwing up. It's a sure-fire bet you'll get something wrong again and I'll be ready and waiting when you do."

"Fuck you, Scully."

"Wonderfully eloquent. I may quote you on that too."

"Be sure that the next time we meet you'll have my knuckles smashing in your teeth."

"I look forward to it. I give as good as I get."

"I won't."

"Something else before I gladly take my leave, Gray. Check out *The Times* as well. Another one of you corrupt buggers takes centre stage."

Gray opened his mouth to protest an innocence he knew didn't exist. A dial tone had already replaced the reporter's voice. Gray swore. The reporter was talented at having the final word.

He turned off his mobile and threw it onto the passenger seat in disgust. He spent half a minute pinching the bridge of his nose to calm down. Scully had that effect on Gray, no matter how hard he tried to stay calm.

Gray logged into the hotel's free Wi-Fi before using his smartphone to access the web browser and searched for Scully's newspaper.

The front page popped up, the lead article by the man himself. The opening paragraphs were lurid in their description, the rest he skimmed.

David Hill's image caught his eye. He'd seen a picture like it a few times in the vicarage. Gray made a note to enquire where Scully had obtained it. Bunged the uniform on the door a few quid to pop inside? Beneath was a shot of the church and another of Arlington House. If he cared to look left, Gray would be able to see the block of flats for himself at pretty much the same angle.

Gray noted the article had been published eleven minutes ago. And there was the statement attested to him, along with an acerbic quip intimating that the force was clueless.

So, Scully had lied. No surprise in that. He'd probably been trying to provoke Gray with the hope he'd spill something, and the article updated accordingly within seconds.

Gray opened another browser page and went to *The Times*. Only limited front page news was available, the detail and interior behind a paywall. Thieving sods.

Gray kicked the car into life. He backed out of the spot, did a quick three-point turn, and headed for the roundabout. When he looked left the tramp had gone. He wondered where he could find a newspaper at this time of night.

Twenty Eight

"Same again?" asked the bartender, nodding at Gray's glass. His skin was marked by eczema, raw and painful looking.

"Works for me."

The barman nodded and worked the pump with his red hands, filling his original glass. Strictly speaking, not allowed these days. Gray didn't care. They were his germs.

The barman pulled a pint of Spitfire. The beer was brown and sported the kind of small head that would drive a northerner mad.

The Chapel was a micropub set up inside a second-hand bookshop because nobody bought paperbacks anymore. Even the pies were bestsellers compared to the novels. There was only Gray and two old blokes in the pub. One had a twinkle in his eye and engaged anyone within shouting distance in conversation. The other made himself unobtrusive. Gray wondered whether he'd spend his retirement in the pub too.

The barman dragged Gray away from the vision of his future by placing the pint on the bar. Gray handed over some cash with one hand, with the other raised the glass and took a gulp of the beer, savouring the hoppy flavour.

"Cheers."

"No problem."

Gray received the shrapnel in change and slid it into his pocket. He returned to his seat in a darkened corner of the pub. The table was dusted with crumbs, the result of Gray's dinner of several packets of crisps (now empty and among the debris).

He'd finally tracked down a copy of *The Times* on the fifth attempt. He'd bought a pack of cigarettes too. Gray needed somewhere to read the paper so headed to the pub, rather than home. Five pages in, he found the story Scully must have been referring to.

Vigilantes Arrested

Police in London arrested five men in the early hours. All were part of a vigilante group involved in hunting paedophiles on-line. The group, calling itself Dark Deeds, apprehended fifty-six-year-old Shaun Gill, jailed for five years for grooming someone he believed to be a thirteen-year-old girl, but was in fact a middle-aged man posing as a minor. It is understood that among the ar-rested men is an as-yet-unnamed Metropolitan Police officer.

Comment, page 14.

Gray flipped to the Comment section. It was a much larger exposé on groups like Dark Deeds. He was surprised to learn how many of them there were – six confirmed, and the author believed yet more were operating under the radar. The vigi-lantes preferred to be thought of as private investigators. The leader of one band rather piously claimed they acted on behalf of concerned parents everywhere, doing what the police were unwilling or unable to do.

The tactic they employed was to set up an online persona as a teenage child, usually a girl, and wait. Before long, some dirty old man would begin grooming the "child", worming their way into their lives, playing on their vulnerabilities, making them dependent. Some of the bolder predators might even ask for photographs or videos. After a while, they'd suggest a meet. And that's when the vigilantes would pounce, restraining the man, fleeing the scene, then notifying police to arrest him.

The text made it clear that the cops themselves were not in favour of this approach, stating it interfered with their own practices and due process. But the public seemed to love it. The average person on the street had few qualms about the methods employed to catch people who preyed on children, particularly since the revelations about Jimmy Savile and the recent wave of disclosures about other notable celebrities and church members. Gray could hardly blame them.

Gray left his jacket on the chair back and pint on the table as place holders, and headed outside. On the narrow pavement he contaminated the fresh air by lighting a cigarette. He pulled out his mobile phone, tapped at the screen as smoke curled from his mouth. The number rang and rang. He was just about to give up when it was answered at last.

Gray introduced himself and asked for Yandell.

"I'm sorry, sir. He's currently unavailable," said a woman who hadn't introduced herself.

"When will he be back?"

"I don't know, sir. I haven't been advised of that."

The comment sounded strange to Gray. "Advised?"

"Yes, sir."

"Is he ill?"

"I couldn't say, sir." It sounded like a strange phrase to Gray.

"Is he suspended?"

"I'm not at liberty to answer. You'll need to speak to my DI." A neat passing of the buck. "But he's not at his desk, sir. Can I ask him to call you?"

Gray gave his details and leisurely finished his cigarette, entering a staring contest with a seagull the size of a dog. He dropped the filter down a nearby drain and went back inside the pub, where he returned to his seat and read the paper in more detail.

"The ghosts of history rapping on your door again?"

Gray didn't need to look up to know it was Carslake.

"Bugger off, sir, and leave me to my melancholy."

"Very poetic." The DCI pulled out a chair opposite Gray and sat down heavily. "And that's no way to speak to a superior officer."

"I'm off-duty." Gray kept his eyes on the newspaper.

Carslake checked his watch. "Actually, you're not."

"So tell HR, or whatever they're called now. How did you know I was here?"

"I guessed."

"Well done. What do you want?"

"The other day I was distracted so I didn't get a chance to ask: how did it go with Doctor Mallory?"

"The best I can say is: it went."

"What am I going to do with you?" asked Carslake after a significant pause.

Gray wanted to tell Carslake everything. About Buckingham, Pennance, McGavin. However, he drained his beer and stood. "Want one?"

"My shout. What are you drinking?"

"As it's on expenses..." Gray tapped his empty glass and sat back down. Carslake headed to the bar to order. A minute later he was back with a pint and a brandy.

"Don't know how you can drink the stuff," said Carslake, pointing at the bitter.

"Practice."

Gray slowly turned a page, willing Carslake to clear off; he could feel the bastard's leaden stare.

"I called the doctor," Carslake said at last.

"Did he talk to you?"

"Of course."

"Whatever happened to patient confidentiality?"

"Mallory said you were belligerent."

"He annoyed me."

"Everyone annoys you."

"I'm doing my job, aren't I?"

"At the moment. I'm concerned things might go backwards again."

Gray stayed quiet.

"Mallory mentioned a prescription," said Carslake.

Gray pulled the bottle out of an inside pocket and rattled the contents.

"Good," said Carslake. "Feeling okay?"

"Fine. I've got to go."

"Pity. I was enjoying our chat."

"The feeling isn't mutual."

Gray stood and gathered his coat, leaving the pint Carslake had purchased untouched. Although Gray really wanted another drink, he couldn't stomach Carslake right now.

"It's all for the best, you'll see," said Carslake.

"Is that what Sylvia said?"

Outside, the wind whistled along Albion Street. Gray fished out his mobile and sent a text to Hamson. It said, "Thanks for dropping me in the shite."

There was an off-licence around the corner. Gray decided to make a pit stop on the way home. It would be a liquid dinner this evening.

Twenty Nine

Gray tossed the paper version of the local rag onto his desk. On the way into the station he'd picked up a copy from the local supermarket.

Scully's article was the lead. At least the photos were less lurid in the black and white print than the full-colour version online.

"I reckon that's me." Fowler, leaning over Gray's shoulder, pointed at the grainy photo of a group in front of St Peter's Church.

Gray's head snapped up. He'd just had a crazy thought. Scully had bribed someone to gain access to the vicarage. Gray had assumed it had been the uniform. But maybe not.

"Do you think it makes me look fat?"

"Fatter," said Hamson.

"This," Gray pointed at the headline, his voice quiet. "Was it you, Fowler?"

"What?"

"Were you responsible for this story?"

Fowler finally got it. The temperature plummeted to sub-zero. Everyone in the room was staring at Gray and Fowler, waiting to see what would happen next.

"I could hardly stop them taking my picture!"

Gray jerked upright. "That's not what I mean, and you know it, you idiot! Have you been talking to the press? There's stuff in there no one else could know!"

Fowler's face reddened. He spoke through his teeth. "You're not seriously suggesting I'm bent, are you?"

"I suppose I am."

"Mike, don't." Hamson grabbed Fowler's arm as he squared up to Gray. Fowler shook her off, moved another step forward. Gray reciprocated, got into Fowler's space.

"Nobody accuses me of being a leak."

"It wouldn't be the first time."

"What's going on here?" The voice came from the doorway.

All eyes shifted from Fowler and Gray to Carslake.

"Just a discussion, sir," said Gray.

"Really?" Carslake flicked his gaze to Fowler.

"Yes," said Fowler, backing away.

"DS Gray, I'd appreciate a word with you," said Carslake. Gray didn't move, eyes firmly on Fowler. "Now."

"We'll take this up later," said Gray.

"Look forward to it," said Fowler.

Gray followed Carslake up the stairs, the latter stepping to one side when they reached Carslake's office, allowing Gray to enter first. Carslake closed the door and leaned on it.

"Would you like to explain to me what the *hell* that was all about?"

Gray ran his fingers through his hair. "It's been a very stressful time."

"Stress has nothing to do with it, Sol. You have to rise above that sort of thing. Railing on a colleague is bad enough, but with Pennance around? What were you thinking?"

Gray felt tired. "I don't know."

"Well, you'd better bloody work it out. And fast. I took you into my confidence the other day. I can't have you blowing it."

Gray shrugged. "What do you want me to say?"

"Get out of here and sort yourself out."

IT DIDN'T TAKE LONG to track down Pennance. He was in the canteen, of all places, seated alone at a table for four, fiddling with his phone. A drink at his elbow. Gray dragged out a chair, sat opposite. He tossed *The Times* across, folded so the vigilante piece was front and centre.

"Know anything about that?" asked Gray.

Pennance barely glanced at it. "It's all over the news."

"You said Yandell was a colleague of sorts."

"Did I?"

"Is it Yandell who's suspended?"

Pennance remained blank. "I've no idea what you're talking about, Sergeant." He pushed the newspaper back across the table and walked away.

Thirty

Five Years Ago

His in-laws arrived in Broadstairs the same day Kate passed on. On hearing the news, they'd packed a bag and travelled the three hours from Malvern. By then, Kate had been transferred to the pathologist for a post-mortem. It would delay the burial.

Kate's father Fred was not a God-fearing man. He was solid, dependable, no-nonsense. Gray liked him. The feeling was not mutual. He and Gray stood in the well-tended garden while Fred's wife Ruth grieved within. Alice was keeping her company.

"Where's Hope?" asked Fred.

"I don't know," said Gray. "She wasn't at school when I went there. Hadn't been all day."

"Playing truant?"

Gray nodded. "Apparently it's been going on for a while."

"And you weren't aware?"

"No."

Fred shook his head. "Hope can't stay with you. Too many bad memories. She'll live with us."

"What if she doesn't want to?"

"I'm sure she'll agree."

"What if I don't agree?"

"Do you really want her?" challenged Fred.

"Yes," said Gray. "She's all I have left."

"Do you have the time and the capacity to look after a teenager?"

Gray didn't answer. It would be a lie if he said "yes".

"As I thought." Fred left Gray alone in the garden. There was packing to be done.

HOPE RETURNED HOME when school finished, as if she'd been there all day. She was surprised to find her grandparents present. Gray told Hope about her mother. At first Hope was unable to say anything. She sat on the end of her bed, totally still. Then tears welled up and rolled down her cheeks.

"Why?" A whisper. "Why?" A shout, then a wail. Hope fell over sideways onto the bed, curled herself up into a ball.

"Your grandparents are here for you. I've packed a bag," Gray paused. "It's best for both of us."

Still Gray kept his emotions suppressed.

When Hope was about to get into Fred's car Gray gave her a hug. She was limp in his arms.

Gray remained silent, trying to convince himself it really *was* for the best. He would see Hope only once more in the next five years.

Thirty-One

The door was double-glazed and inset with a mosaic pattern. Gray rapped on it.

It was a nice place, a big house, newly built on what used to be convent grounds on the outskirts of Broadstairs. When the wind was blowing in the right direction it'd be a strong bet you'd be able to hear the waves.

After another knock, the door opened. A face peered out, most of the body hidden by the door.

"Hello, Margaret," said Gray. "I'm here for that follow-up."

Margaret said nothing, simply walked inside. He followed her into the living room. She sat on the edge of a high-backed chair, leaning forward slightly, her hands clamped together between her knees. The space was cluttered, sofa and chairs, dining table, cushions, plants, bowls of potpourri, china dolls, crockery, books, and several crucifixes. No Christmas decorations. Perhaps Margaret focused all of her time on St Peter's Church.

There wasn't anywhere for him to sit, so Gray fetched a chair from a nearby dining table. It reminded him of the church pew, hard and uncomfortable. Perhaps the Fowlers didn't like having dinner parties or eating together. Margaret, however, sat back, adopting a more relaxed pose.

"What do you want?" she asked.

"I have some questions."

"Fire away."

"When did you last see Reverend Hill alive?"

"The evening before Alice found him. I went to the service."

"By yourself?"

"Of course. You know Mike thinks it's all mumbo jumbo."

Gray kept his views to himself. "How did David seem?"

"Absolutely fine. There was nothing different about him. I'd been with him and Alice for most of the day, finishing off the Christmas decorations."

"What did you do when you left the church?"

"I came straight home. I watched television all evening."

"Alone?"

"Thankfully I'm never truly alone. Because of God. He fills my world."

"What about Mike?"

"If my husband ever felt something for me it withered years ago. I'm just opportune, this house simply somewhere to sleep, eat, shower, and very occasionally have sex. Not much of an existence, is it?"

Gray didn't know what to say. Fowler never spoke about his personal life and Gray's own contact with them as a couple had been minimal to non-existent for a decade. He'd always thought they were happy.

"Sorry, am I oversharing?" She didn't look sorry. "David, Alice, and God are everything to me because I have nothing else. The police force has taken it all."

Margaret looked infinitely sad. It was a fleeting emotion, a flicker over her face.

"Have you ever seen this person?" Gray showed Margaret the photograph of Buckingham, trying to get back on track. The photo was beginning to get tatty, the corners folded, edges worn.

"No."

"Are you sure? Around the church, perhaps?"

"No, definitely not. We don't have much trouble with vandals these days."

Gray didn't correct Margaret's misinterpretation.

"Cup of tea?" she said. "It's always the solution." A wan smile spread across her face. She and Alice shared several common traits, a tea fixation being one of them.

"Yes, thanks. Can I use your toilet?"

Margaret told Gray where the bathroom was. He used it, washed and dried his hands.

When he re-entered the living room he froze. Margaret was sitting in the chair again, legs crossed, arms on the rest, wearing only matching red underwear. He looked away. Her outer clothes lay in a neat pile on the floor beside her.

"I've always been attracted to you, Sol," she whispered.

"Get dressed, Margaret."

"Don't you want me?"

"It's a sin, Margaret. We both know it. God knows it."

"You don't care about God!" snapped Margaret, her face switching from misery to fury.

"Please, get dressed." Gray picked up her discarded clothes and held them out, his face averted.

"Am I that disgusting to look at?"

He didn't answer.

The clothes were snatched from his fingers. "You can see yourself out."

Gray heard footsteps and when he glanced over his shoulder, Margaret was nowhere in sight. He'd be keeping the details of this particular interview to himself...

GRAY FOUND ALICE AT home. Not in her house, at the church. She was carefully watering the Christmas tree. Alice caught sight of Gray when she straightened up. Her expression changed immediately.

"Are you here to ridicule me again, Sergeant?" she asked. "Because if so, I have nothing to say."

Gray held up the photograph. "Do you recognise this person?"

Alice frowned. "May I?"

Gray nodded and she took the image, peered at it.

"This is the poor soul who threw himself off Arlington House earlier in the week," she said. "I saw it in the newspaper."

"Yes."

"Is he connected to David?"

"That's what I'm attempting to determine. His name was Nick Buckingham. Have you seen him around the church at all?"

"No, never."

"Are you sure?"

"I may be old, but my mind is perfectly clear."

"That wasn't what I meant."

"You implied it."

Gray sighed. "I apologise if I offended you. It wasn't intentional."

Alice handed over Buckingham's mugshot. "As usual, it's too late to take it back. If there's nothing else, maybe you should leave."

Gray nodded and let himself out.

Thirty Two

Gray's eyes opened. Darkness. He yawned, rubbed his face, felt his palm scraped by stubble. Theoretically he'd slept, but he didn't feel refreshed.

From arriving home, and through the wee small hours, Gray had sat on the floor of his attic room shuffling the casework on Tom's disappearance into neat little piles until he could keep his eyes open no longer. Like painting the Forth Road Bridge, it was a never-ending task.

Gray swung his legs out of bed, padded barefoot down the stairs. He turned on the shower and suffered a brief soaking in the gloom. After a rapid towelling to dry himself, he filled the sink with cold water, scraped at his chin with a disposable razor.

The blade seemed to have no noticeable effect on his face; it still felt rough to the touch. He emptied the sink and watched the water disappear.

That's where my life has gone. Down the plughole.

Actually, it went there years ago, countered a second voice.

Kate.

"You're dead," said Gray out loud to his pale reflection in the mirror. It stared back at him, unmoved. A cold breeze through the partially open bathroom door sent a shiver down his spine. Christ, things were getting bad when he started talking to his dead wife.

Time to get dressed. His wrinkled dark blue suit was lying over the back of a chair where he'd thrown it last night. He pulled on yesterday's shirt after a brief sniff of the armpit revealed no residual odour, and followed up with a tie. He gave in to wearing clean underwear. He had some standards, after all.

He pulled on trousers, shrugged on a jacket, grabbed his mobile and warrant card and slipped them into a pocket. He nipped back into the bathroom for a spray of deodorant. After a second's thought, he applied another couple of blasts to his shirt to be on the safe side.

Gray took the winding route to the station. As he passed Café Tanya, Gray slowed and glanced at his watch. Although it was still early the lights were on and he could do with a decent brew.

Why not?

A few hundred yards along, Gray found a rare parking space. A sleet shower started the moment he stepped out of the car and he turned his collar up against it. When he reached the café he saw a sign on the door that said "Closed."

Tanya was inside, lifting chairs down from tables. She paused at Gray's knock and grinned. Gray could detect genuine warmth through the glass as she unlocked the door.

"Lovely to see you again, Sol."

"And you, Tanya."

She stepped out of the way to allow him entry. "First customer of the day."

"So I can come in?"

"As it's you." Tanya wiped her hands on her apron and moved behind the counter, her smile not diminishing in the slightest.

"I wanted to thank you for the coffee and apologise for running off like that."

"I'm not offended. The law beckoned. What happened?"

"A murder."

"The vicar?" Gray nodded. "I saw it on the news. Let me make you a coffee. You probably need one."

"I just bought something supposed to be coffee but it was awful. A proper one would be great, thanks."

Tanya checked the temperature of the silver brute of a coffee machine with a tentative pat. "It still needs a few more minutes, unless you prefer yours lukewarm?"

"God, no. I've had enough drinks that have gone cold to last me a lifetime."

Tanya laughed, stepped away from the counter, and took a seat at the nearest table, subliminally inviting Gray to follow suit. He sat down but couldn't think of a thing to say.

"How's work?" asked Tanya.

"The usual."

"You're looking stressed."

"That's observant."

"Part of the job."

"Like remembering everyone's order?"

"Exactly like that."

"So what else do you observe, Detective Tanya?"

Leaning forward, knuckles on chin, Tanya narrowed her eyes, searching his face. Eventually she said, "Loneliness, sadness, hope."

"That's an interesting combination." Gray was jolted, despite himself.

"Am I right?"

"I can neither confirm nor deny your assertions."

"You sound like a lawyer off the TV."

"Unfortunately, I know one or two." Gray thought of Neil Wright and his mind drifted onto Buckingham again.

"Penny for them."

He pushed Buckingham to the back of his mind for now. Gray's phone rang. He checked the screen. "Excuse me, I have to take this."

"No problem. I'll get your coffee. To go?"

"Unfortunately." He nodded and answered the phone: "DS Gray."

"Morning, Sol," said Dr Clough. "How are we this fine day?"

A glance out of the steamed-up window revealed it to be anything other than fine. "Marvellous."

"Glad to hear it. Look, sorry to call you so early. I wanted to let you know Buckingham's tox results are in. I've sent you a copy."

"What're the highlights?"

"Appropriate word choice. He was loaded with cocaine. The levels measured were very high and clearly he would have been too."

"Until he came crashing down."

"Quite. I thought you'd like to know as soon as possible. I'm aware how important this case is to you." Another unexpected piece of intuition.

Clough didn't do small talk so, message delivered, he rang off, his work done. Gray considered the additional information. Could Buckingham have simply fallen? Possibly, given his consumption of narcotics. Although that didn't explain the bruising. Gray slid the phone back in his pocket. He turned back to Tanya. "I've got to go."

"No problem." She slid a paper cup across the counter, plastic lid firmly in place. When Gray went for his wallet Tanya said, "It's on the house."

"That's very kind. You'll have to let me return the favour and buy you a drink some time."

"Are you asking me out on a date, Detective?"

"I didn't mean it to sound like that."

"That's okay, I don't mind. And yes."

"Yes?"

"I'll happily let you buy me a drink."

"Oh."

"That's it? Oh?"

"I'm just surprised."

"Don't be. I'm desperate."

"Oh."

Tanya laughed. "You should see your face. I'm joking. About being desperate, that is. I really would like to go out for a drink some time."

"Great. I'll give you a call to fix something up."

"Then I better give you my number." She picked up one of her takeaway paper cups and in black marker scrawled her number on the outside. She slid Gray's cup inside it. "You won't forget now, will you?"

THERE WERE, IN FACT, two reports waiting for Gray on his arrival at the station. The first, Buckingham's toxicological analysis, was attached to an email from Clough.

He skimmed through the couple of pages and settled on the relevant information that was contained in just a handful of lines:

Presence of significant quantities of Class A drug, subsequently identified as cocaine.

The printer whirred to life at Gray's command. One copy of the tox report for Pennance, who was on the phone at Hamson's desk, and the other for himself.

Gray went back to his inbox. At the top of the list was a new, unread message. It appeared to be spam. Gray almost deleted it, until he noticed with a jolt the sender was apparently Nick Buckingham.

He double clicked the message. There wasn't any text, just a JPEG attachment. Gray glanced around to make sure no one was watching before he clicked the file, opening up a new window.

A photo of a man, if the hairy arm was anything to go by, and a youth filled his screen. The man appeared to be undressing, the kid was already naked, a bored expression on his face. Only the man's back was visible, impossible to tell who he was. There was a small smudge on his left shoulder. A birth mark or a tattoo? Either the picture had been cropped, or the man was too close to the camera.

Gray recognised two aspects immediately.

The kid. The location.

Buckingham. The flat in Arlington House.

No one was paying Gray any attention, and Hamson was nowhere in sight. He sent the printer whirring again.

Pennance was off the phone now. "Sir?" said Gray. "Have you got a moment?"

The DI came over to Gray's desk. "What's up Sol?"

"You're the IT whizz kid, what do you make of this?" Gray tapped his computer screen.

"Jesus," whispered Pennance, noting the time stamp. "Nick couldn't have sent it, he was already dead."

"Who would do this?"

"No idea, but if you forward me the email, I might be able to trace it."

Gray sent the email to Pennance, then collected the documents from the printer. With any luck, Pennance would be able to shed some light on the photo and its sender.

GRAY FOUND HAMSON IN the incident room where activity was a little calmer than the previous day, that initial adrenalin-loaded rush of a new case dissipated with time and effort.

"Ballistics," she said by way of greeting and Gray received his second report of the morning. The critical material was even more scant than Clough's. The bullets were badly damaged. The evaluation determined they were 200 grain, .38 Special projectiles. The bad news was the ammunition was very common and relatively easily sourced. However, the Special version was exclusively designed for revolvers. Which explained why no casings had been discovered at the scene.

"I've just received this," said Gray, handing Hamson a copy of the photo.

She stared at it, then at Gray, appearing as stunned as he felt.

"Who sent it?"

"The email said it was from Buckingham himself. Pennance is looking into it now."

"There you are," said Pennance from the open doorway. He sauntered over to Hamson and Gray.

"Any luck?" asked Gray.

Pennance shook his head. "Whoever encrypted the email is better than me. I do have a friend who may be able to help," he paused. "If you're okay with that?"

"Do it," said Hamson. "Why would somebody send this to you? And why now?"

"Maybe we're not making fast enough progress?" Gray shrugged.

Pennance interrupted. "Anyways, I've been taking a look at the reverend's online activity."

"Anything? Or is that a bust too?" Hamson asked.

"Initially, nothing out of the ordinary. He only used his social media presence to promote the church. Then I found this."

Pennance handed over a printout of a newspaper article from a few months back. Written by Scully.

"Local Vicar Fights Online Abuse," read Gray out loud. He skimmed the commentary, which was about the Reverend David Hill fighting his own good fight, wanting a pornography ban and lambasting Internet service providers for allowing adult content to be so freely available.

"I got access to his browser history via his ISP. Seems Reverend Hill was on a crusade after all," said Pennance. "And I rang all the local PC repair shops."

"I asked a DC to do that," Hamson cut in, her voice sharp. "Lazy little bugger."

"That was down to me. I took over."

"Even so..."

"And?" asked Gray.

"Nothing."

"Bloody hell, Marcus," said Hamson. "After all that build-up?"

"I mean no one I spoke to had a computer brought in by Reverend Hill or Mrs Newbold."

"Where is it, then?"

But any further discussion of the computer was interrupted when Fowler stormed into the incident room. "What the hell have you done to my wife?" he shouted, and launched himself at Gray.

Thirty Three

Compared to the hard lines of the interview rooms, the comfort suites were designed to put the victim at ease. Alice Newbold and Margaret Fowler contrasted perfectly. Whereas Alice sat upright, all straight back and indignation, Margaret was slumped over, bent and defeated. Neither looked particularly at ease.

And neither did Hamson, who was conducting the interview.

Gray hadn't been allowed to join the interview and instead he watched and listened just along the corridor via a computer monitor. He still ached from hitting the floor after Fowler charged at him, but thankfully was otherwise uninjured.

"This is a very serious allegation," said Hamson. "Attempted rape."

"It is," said Alice. "I want Sergeant Gray arrested immediately."

It took all Gray's mental strength not to storm into the room and rip Alice's head off.

"The alleged attack by the suspect was on Mrs Fowler, though."

"That's right."

Margaret gave an almost imperceptible shake of the head.

"Mrs Fowler is so traumatised by the incident she's unable to speak. I'm here to represent her."

"When did the alleged attack occur?"

"There's nothing *alleged* about it, Inspector. It happened yesterday!"

Margaret shook her head once more.

"Margaret, we'll need to collect evidence."

"Evidence?" said Margaret, her voice tiny.

"Yes. We'd like to collect various samples. We have a kit to do so. Urine and a vaginal swab so we can check for semen."

"Semen?"

"And alcohol or drugs."

"Why?"

"Large quantities of alcohol or drugs could determine whether you were capable of consent."

"Oh. We just drank tea."

"If possible, Mrs Fowler, I need you to not go to the toilet until we've collected samples. The same goes for eating, drinking, or smoking."

"I don't smoke."

"Disgusting habit," said Alice.

"From here I'll be stepping out of the process."

"Why?" asked Margaret.

"We have specially trained officers to take you through the judicial process."

"This will go to court?"

"If there's sufficient evidence, then yes."

"I don't want that."

"Yes, you do!" snapped Alice.

"No!" Margaret stood abruptly, faced Hamson. "I don't wish to take this any further, Inspector. It's not right." Margaret lowered her head so her eyes were looking at the table.

"What isn't, Mrs Fowler?" asked Hamson.

There was a long pause while Margaret gathered herself. "I just wanted to have sex, that's all. It's been so long since Mike and I did anything. I needed the appreciation of a man and Sol was there. It was a stupid, stupid impulse and I was embarrassed by my behaviour.

"Alice came round to see me, and she asked me what was wrong. I pretended Sol and I had had sex. Alice insisted he must have forced himself on me. She told me I should make a complaint to the police. She wouldn't take no for an answer."

Alice glared at Margaret.

"I'm sorry, Alice," said Margaret.

Alice stood and left the comfort suite.

"I apologise for causing any trouble," said Margaret. "Arrest me if you wish."

WHEN GRAY ENTERED CARSLAKE'S office, Hamson and Fowler were already seated. At the sight of Gray, Fowler pushed himself out of his chair and lurched at Gray who squared up to take the assault head-on.

"DS Fowler!" barked Carslake, stopping Fowler in his tracks. "Sit down!"

Fowler stood his ground, forcing Carslake to repeat himself. Fowler only sat again when Hamson took hold of his arm and said, "Hear what he has to say."

"She's lying," said Gray, taking a seat. "She said so herself."

"Margaret always tells the truth," said Fowler.

"Tell us your side of the story, Sol. It's important Mike hears it for himself."

"I went round to ask Margaret about Reverend Hill and she propositioned me."

"Bullshit!" shouted Fowler. Hamson put a hand on Fowler's forearm. He shook it off.

"Let him finish," said Carslake.

"I went to the bathroom while Margaret made some tea. When I returned she was in her underwear. She asked me for sex, I asked her to get dressed. If Margaret had been subjected to an examination, nothing would have been found, because nothing happened. Whether you like it or not, Mike, I'm telling the truth."

"Oh my God," said Fowler. He wiped a hand over his face.

"Are you satisfied with Sol's explanation, Mike?" asked Carslake.

"I need to talk to Margaret."

"We've charged both Alice and Margaret with wasting police time. We had to."

Fowler stood up.

"Mike," said Hamson, but he walked out of the room.

"Go on," said Carslake, giving her permission to go after him.

When they were alone, Gray said, "It's absolutely what happened, Jeff."

"She's not pressing charges, so that's what counts."

Gray couldn't quite comprehend what he'd just heard. "Nothing happened!"

"If you say so. It's a dead end now. Unless Margaret changes her mind."

"For Christ's sake, Jeff, I'm innocent."

"I believe you."

But Gray didn't believe Carslake. When he left the office, Sylvia gave him an even dirtier look than usual.

In the gents along the corridor from Carslake's office Gray splashed cold water from the tap onto his face, ran wet fingers through his hair. He looked up as the bathroom door opened and Hamson stepped inside, shutting the door behind her. Gray turned around, leaned against the sink. "Mike's gone home," she said.

"That's not going to be an easy discussion," said Gray. "How is he?"

"Angry and blaming you."

"Great. Just what I need."

"And we're all going out for a drink later."

"Mike's still coming along tonight?"

"I'm trying to persuade him."

Alcohol and anger, thought Gray. *What a great combination.*

Thirty Four

"**C**ome on, Sol!" said Hamson.

It was time for the dreaded birthday pub crawl and Gray was pretending to be on the phone again, faking an animated conversation with the speaking clock. The build-up to the main event had been underway all day, Hamson's deliberations increasing in frequency as the event neared.

She accosted and cajoled every cop who crossed her path – beaming at them when they accepted the invite (again) or pulling a pout when they turned her down.

With half an hour to go Hamson got changed in the women's toilets, selecting something a little more daring than her work clothes, and spent the intervening period perfecting her make-up in the detectives' office.

As the shift's conclusion crawled ever nearer and Hamson's excitement grew, so did Gray's desolation. Hamson coerced her colleagues once more to ensure her popularity. While the clock ticked, the office filled with fellow partygoers. DI Pennance and even Brian bloody Blake were included.

At the top of the hour Hamson beckoned to Gray, mimed drinking. He shook his head, mouthed, "Important call." Incredulity splashed across Hamson's face.

Ever the gentleman, Pennance jumped to aid the damsel in distress, striding over to Gray's desk and holding out his hand for the phone. Gray ended the call before Pennance reached him. "They rang off," said Gray.

"That was fortunate. Looks like you can join everyone now."

"First round's on you," said Hamson.

"Great."

GRAY STOOD AT THE BAR of the Britannia, trying to avoid leaning against the bar top, which was dripping wet. The Britannia was a low-slung establishment sporting a fort-like appearance typical of the area. The attempt failed. No one cared about faux history.

Its major draw was proximity: the pub stood across the road from the Winter Gardens, a once-popular entertainment venue sunk into the chalk cliff, and the police station. The Britannia was next door to the latter; it took seconds to clock off from one shift and clock on to another.

The interior swelled with bodies and commotion at the cops' entrance, a hubbub of joviality and anticipated excess with Hamson at the centre and loving every moment of it.

Pennance had effectively escorted Gray to the pub. Pennance stood with his back to the bar, watching the unfolding frivolity. Slade's "Merry Xmas Everybody" hammered through the speakers.

"Your lot certainly know how to enjoy themselves." Pennance shouted in an effort to be heard over the guitarist's simplistic yet catchy riff.

"Why do you think I was trying to avoid the festivities?"

"You're a miserable bugger."

"Never pretended to be anything else."

A cheer went up and Gray glanced over his shoulder. DCI Carslake was threading his way through the crowd, Sylvia and Blake behind him. Carslake nodded at Pennance, who made space for him. His secretary hung back a pace.

"Bit of a surprise seeing you here, Jeff."

"Couldn't resist when I heard your wallet was getting an airing," said Carslake. "It's been a while."

"My sides are splitting." Gray narrowed his eyes. "Is that lipstick on your cheek?"

"What?" Carslake rubbed at a smudge of red. "Yvonne's doing, that."

"Your secret's safe with me."

"I'm relieved."

It seemed that every other cop on the island had heard about it being Gray's round by the numbers merrily ordering alcohol and pointing at him. He suspected some of them were still on duty. Blake ordered a lager, Sylvia a gin and tonic.

"I just hope they take credit cards," said Gray.

"We do," replied the barman, pulling another pint. A colleague was assembling a line of shot glasses and pouring a clear spirit into each, ready to be deposited into the lager.

"In that case, make mine a double scotch," said Carslake.

Gray suspected it was going to be a long night. And an expensive one.

"Cheers, Sol," said Pennance, raising a pint in salute. Sylvia scurried off, drink in hand, without so much as a thank you.

"You're welcome," said Gray to her back.

SEVERAL HOURS LATER, the night well in progress, Gray was loitering outside the latest destination, The Frog and something. The pub crawl had reached the Old Town's square and almost reached the roughest pub in Margate, The English Flag. The landlord was a dick, but Gray had managed to save them from what would have been a challenging encounter with the locals, steering them here instead. It was a good job someone had remained relatively sober.

Gray was cold. He didn't care. Better to be outside in the elements than stuck in the middle of Hamson's celebration. He had a drink in his hand.

The door swung back, liberating a blast of noise from within. A shriek from Hamson, a bellowed laugh from Blake, the blast of sickeningly cheerful seasonal music. Pennance emerged from the pub. Just when Gray thought the evening couldn't get any worse.

"Not enjoying the party?" Pennance asked.

"Not really."

"Me neither."

A group of carousers entered the square, women dressed in bright outfits and pointy hats, all of them holding balloons. Hen party or Christmas party paraphernalia, it was difficult to tell. They made their way over to the pub and spilled inside. Right on cue, a huge cheer went up, from both groups.

Pennance said, "We haven't really had the opportunity to speak."

"We've had plenty, DI Pennance," said Gray. "You've just been unwilling to engage."

"I meant on a personal level. And please, call me Marcus."

"I'll stick with the formalities, thanks."

"Suit yourself."

"I will."

"I can understand how frustrating it is for someone to come down from another force and take over your investigation."

"Believe it or not, DI Pennance, I'll be delighted whenever you get to the bottom of whatever well you're looking down. What I don't like is being kept in the dark."

"It's... necessary."

"Right." Carslake's prediction returned to Gray, that perhaps Pennance wasn't here for Buckingham at all. Could he trust him? "One question."

"Fire away, though I may not be able to answer." Pennance smiled thinly.

"Is it corruption?"

Pennance stared at Gray. "Not as far as I know."

"I don't believe you."

Gray was about to ask a question that would connect the Reverend Hill and Nick Buckingham when the pub door opened again. Both men twisted towards the movement. Framed in the doorway was Tanya, stunning in a scarlet dress.

"Fancy meeting you here," she said to Gray, and smiled at Pennance in an effort at politeness. Gray liked her even more for it.

"Hello," said Gray. He tried to sound nonchalant, wasn't sure it came off.

Pennance checked his watch. "I'd better be getting off anyway. I'll catch up with you tomorrow, Sol."

Gray nodded. If Pennance was anticipating some thanks in the morning for clearing off he'd have a bloody long wait.

Pennance left and Tanya moved towards Gray, joining him in leaning against the wall which offered partial shelter from the wind.

"You two don't seem to like each other," said Tanya.

"Me and Pennance? What makes you think that?"

"The atmosphere out here, I'd have struggled to cut it with one of my sharpest knives."

"It's complicated."

"Usually is."

"Yes."

"I guess all that lot inside are with you?"

"Sort of. Part of my team."

"Having fun?"

"Not really." The alcohol intake and Pennance's guarded behaviour afforded him an unusual amount of honesty and openness. Gray was feeling pretty drunk. "A colleague's birthday party. She's my boss, so no choice really."

"Same here on the choice bit. Hen do for my niece."

"The bunch that went in a minute ago?"

"My worst nightmare. Drunk women out on the pull, egging each other on."

"Does that include you?" Gray kicked himself as soon as the words passed his lips, felt Tanya's eyes boring into him. "Sorry, that just slipped out."

"Pass me a cigarette and I may forgive you."

"How about I buy you that drink?"

"Now you're pushing it."

"Worth a try."

"Always." She smiled. "Do you enjoy being a policeman?"

"Enjoy? It's not really a word I'd associate with the job. Most of the time I'm dealing with tragedy."

"That explains why it sometimes looks like you've got the weight of the universe on your shoulders when you come into my café."

"Didn't we have this discussion earlier?"

"We never finished it. Humour me."

"A lot of bad things have happened around me. Still do."

"You're hardly talking me into that drink."

"Sorry."

"And off you go again, apologising."

Gray opened his mouth. His brain vetoed any further apologies. He closed his mouth again.

"There, we're making progress," said Tanya.

For the third time the pub door opened. Hamson came out into the square, pulling up short when she clocked Gray. Her eyes flicked to Tanya. "I just came outside to see where you were, make sure you're okay."

"I'm fine, Von, thanks."

"Are you going to introduce me?"

The pub door crashed open. Fowler, obviously drunk, staggered out and put an arm around Hamson. "Look who it is."

"I told you to stay inside," said Hamson.

"What's wrong with saying hello to my old friend, Solomon?" Fowler sneered.

"Nothing happened, Mike. I swear it," said Gray.

"That's what she says too. I don't know what to believe any more."

"Let me buy you a beer."

"I don't want anything from you. Bastard. It was all okay until you came along. We had an understanding."

"That's enough, Mike," said Hamson. She turned around and thrust a palm at Fowler's chest until they were back indoors.

"What was all that about?" asked Tanya.

"Just work stuff. It's a long story."

"Do you want to talk about it?"

"Not really."

"She's attractive."

"Yvonne? I suppose."

"Do you want that drink, then?"

Gray was taken aback. He thought he'd blown it. "Sure."

"Not here, though. I'd never hear the end of it from my lot. They'd want to know all about you. Can I have a moment to get my coat?"

The wait was a nervous one, and one during which Gray grew increasingly convinced that she'd stood him up, that this was all a big joke she was sharing with her mates at his expense. He was about to leave and get a taxi, rather than face the shame of facing a flock of laughing women, when the door swung open again.

"My turn to apologise this time," said Tanya. "The girls were trying to persuade me to stay. The bastards hid my handbag." She held up an arm, a coat draped over it and black bag on her wrist.

"That's okay. I didn't mind the wait."

"You're a bit out of practice at this, aren't you?"

"What?"

"Talking to women."

"You can tell?"

"It's okay. I don't mind giving you some guidance."

"Thanks. Where do you want to go?"

"Well away from here."

"Works for me."

"Are you going to say goodbye to your friends?"

"They won't notice I've gone."

"Where do you live?"

"Broadstairs."

"We're neighbours then. We could go back to yours?"

"To my house?" he asked, worrying about the crudity of his decor, hardly a great advert for a prospective partner.

"I was thinking of a pub? Somewhere near both of us?"

Gray kicked himself, yet again getting ahead of himself. "Good. That's what I was thinking too."

"You sound relieved."

"Not at all!"

Tanya eyed Gray, gave him a wry half-smile.

"I'll call for a taxi," he said.

"I'd prefer to walk and find one. I could do with some fresh air. I'm feeling pretty pissed."

"Into the New Town, then."

As Gray started to walk across the square he felt Tanya fall into step beside him. A moment later her hand slid into the crook of his left arm.

The decision to go straight home was made by Tanya somewhere between Margate and Broadstairs.

"What's your address?" she asked Gray.

Gray told her and she relayed the location to the driver, who nodded. Ten minutes later, Gray was struggling to close the front door with his foot while returning Tanya's passionate kiss.

THE INTRUDING SUNLIGHT woke Gray. He hadn't closed the curtains, too distracted last night. Silence. He raised his head, tentatively glanced over. The bed was empty, although a depression in the mattress and the hint of residual heat remained to prove it hadn't been a dream.

He rolled over. A glance onto the floor showed him Tanya's clothes were gone. She must have slid out while he was sleeping. There wasn't a note in sight. Maybe she'd left one downstairs. Gray hoped her departure wasn't due to embarrassment. He lay back on the pillow, resolved to have five minutes to properly arouse. He smiled at the word association, and at the good memory he'd always possess.

IT WAS LATE MORNING when Gray's mobile rang from somewhere on the floor. He should find it, but couldn't be bothered. Everyone was allowed a day off, weren't they? It would stop soon enough.

It did.

The chime kicked in again, finally pushing Gray from under his duvet. His head was pounding. He crawled across the floor, hunting for the phone.

He found it in the pocket of his scrunched-up, inside-out trousers.

"Hello," he said.

"About bloody time!" barked Hamson.

"What's up?"

"You're needed. There's a body."

Thirty Five

F ive Years Ago
It was a beautiful, sunny day. Cold, but bright. Rain would fit Gray's mood, and the occasion, much better.

A few of the congregation had demanded that the burial could not proceed because Kate had taken her own life. But Alice Newbold had silenced even the most fervently negative voices.

The service went smoothly, the arrangements apparently made by Kate only a few weeks previously. Gray wanted to ask Alice and Hill whether they knew of his wife's plans. Not now. After.

The reverend's supple voice floated across the surprisingly large number of mourners who'd turned out. A small number of Gray's colleagues showed their support - people Kate couldn't stand, like Carslake and Fowler - as well as the church-goers who had prayed with Gray's wife on an almost daily basis.

But the true believers were fewer each year as, one by one, old age or disease whittled away at their number. Scully was in the congregation too. Not for support, but for a story.

And Hope. All Gray could do was smile a hello at her. His in-laws, now her guardians, kept her away from him. Every time he glanced their way, Gray was met by a wall of hate.

Gray scanned the crowd, concentrating on the spaces be-tween the bodies because he'd be smaller than the adults. Looking for him. For Tom. He ignored the fact that Tom was ten and had been missing five years.

The coffin passed, led by Hill en route to the burial plot. Past the stones arranged to face the church. They looked like a crowd of pale beings, preparing to accept another wasted spirit into the afterlife.

The Fowlers were at his back, Jeff Carslake at his shoulder, proving once more he was the best of friends by not saying a word. He was there if needed.

The gravesite was at the furthest reaches of church land. Few burials occurred now; there simply wasn't the space. Another reason why some objected. Perhaps they were worried their own bodies wouldn't fit when the time came.

Next to Hill was the place of honour, at the head of the abyss. Gray filled the gap. The onlookers duly arranged themselves in a circle around the grave. The coffin was slowly lowered. Gray threw some soil on top; a thud as it hit expensive wood. The dirt marked his palm. He didn't wipe it away.

When all was said and nothing constructive had been done, the mourners drifted away in knots, some fast, some slow. They were unsure how to behave. Carslake dealt with them in Gray's mental absence.

Tom was not here. Gray had been looking every day since he'd disappeared. It was then that Gray dropped to his knees beside his wife's grave, beside Tom's grave and began to cry among the gravestones. For Kate, for Tom. For Hope, too. But not for himself.

He deserved nobody's sympathy.

Thirty Six

I n a heartbeat Gray was dressed and on the move, his warrant card in his pocket. He patted his pockets for his wallet, but couldn't find it. Must have left it in the pub last night. A patrol car waited outside, Gray's own vehicle still parked at the back of the station. The car took him down the hill towards the sea, unrestrained by traffic at this time of day.

The pleasure of those few hours with Tanya was suddenly overshadowed by the prospect of investigating yet another death. First Nick Buckingham. Then Reverend Hill. Now a third victim. Gray wondered if he was getting too old for all this stuff.

A switchback single track dropped at a steep angle down the chalk cliff onto the esplanade, a long strip of cast concrete that traversed the beaches. From Louisa Bay, around the horseshoe-shaped Viking Bay, and out towards the lesser sands of Broadstairs. The car pulled up at Stone Bay. Silent at this time of year. Beach huts flat packed, café closed for the winter, the stretch now dedicated to dog walkers and fitness freaks.

A salty wind picked at Gray's clothes as he exited the warmth of the car. He buttoned his coat up to the neck. The cliff towered above him, flecks of flint in the chalk making the expanse look like a row of teeth, tainted with decay. Higher still, seagulls wheeled, sinuous curves propelled by gusts of wind.

Hamson and Fowler stood in a tight huddle, perhaps sharing body heat. A female police constable with a woman and a dog were yards further along. The rhythmic pounding of the sea provided a white noise accompaniment as Hamson threw an impatient wave at Gray and he forced his leaden feet into motion.

As he approached, Fowler nudged his chin up in a minimal greeting, clearly still unhappy. Gray wasn't in the mood to apologise for something he hadn't done.

Fowler strained at a cigarette, cupped behind a hand to shield it from the wind. He was green in the face, his eyes milky, like a rotting fish. Gray felt himself needing a cigarette. He slapped the yearning into submission. Hamson, when she walked over, appeared no worse for wear.

A cordon of police tape fluttered erratically, a couple of constables stood sentry at the crime scene, covering the east and west.

"Where did you get to last night?" said Hamson eventually.

"Home, Von. I'd had enough."

"You missed a really good end to the evening."

"I'll live." He felt sick. "Maybe."

"Speaking of which, good job it's out of season."

In the height of summer this part of the Kent coast would be teeming with visitors, drawn like iron filings to a magnet by the quaint Dickensian feel of the town and its pristine beaches.

"Where's the body? Still in situ?"

Fowler nodded. "Behind the rocks over there."

"Who found it?"

"Dog walker. Mrs Brenda Bates."

"She's been interviewed?"

"Yes, there's a PC with her now."

"Forensics are here." Fowler nodded at a white van making slow progress down to the beach. The driver was exercising extreme caution in case the van plunged the few feet onto the sand and exploded.

The van crawled past Gray and halted a few feet beyond. It disgorged two men, one of whom was Brian Blake. The other Gray didn't recognise.

"Has anyone viewed the body yet?" said Blake to Gray, acknowledging Hamson only with a curled lip and minimal nod. To Blake's mind, Gray was the lesser of two evils.

"As I'm the SIO," said Hamson, "I'll answer your question. DS Gray has only just arrived on the scene."

No argument was forthcoming from Blake. "As you wish," he said stiffly, his face redder than usual.

"Nobody has been near the corpse since the woman who discovered it."

"Well, at least one of you got something right."

"I don't appreciate the insinuation of incompetence."

"That's an assumption on your part. Can you bring me up to speed?"

Hamson crossed her arms. "Say please."

"What?" said Blake.

She remained impassive. "A bit of politeness never hurt anyone."

"For God's sake, will you *please* inform me of your findings to date!"

"That's more like it. I'd be delighted to." It took a couple of minutes for Hamson to recount Bates's discovery. There was a pregnant pause at the conclusion.

"What?" said Blake.

"She's expecting a thank you," said Gray.

"Then DI Hamson will be waiting a bloody long time!" Blake's colleague was trying, and failing, to suppress a grin as the CSM turned his ire elsewhere. "Get taking some bloody photos!"

Blake stalked around to the back of the van and threw the doors open. He handed out the obligatory gear.

"Let's go, then," said Blake and led Gray down concrete steps and onto the sand. The wall was shaped like a backwards question mark, designed to rebuff the sea. It didn't always work.

The beach itself was a gentle incline to the surf. The task of walking was somewhat harder on the softer sand untouched by the water, easier on the damp stuff.

The body, clearly a woman, lay face down well below the peak water mark, indicated by a straggly contour of washed-up debris. Dark hair splayed out from the corpse's skull as if it had received an electric shock, fragments of seaweed were tangled within the strands. Pale, bare limbs poked out from a scarlet dress. One flat shoe adorned a foot, the other bare.

No, it couldn't be...

He ran to the body, ignoring Hamson's shout, knelt, gently brushed the hair from the woman's face as he had just hours previously. A lifeless green eye stared back at him.

Thirty Seven

Gray leaned forward and peered through the windscreen at Tanya's house. It was three-quarters of the way along Alexandra Road, a narrow and quiet cul-de-sac in Broadstairs. Only a few streets and a few minutes' walk from where she was found.

The construction was of brick and flint, older than his own, Victorian, when attitudes were solid and dependable, not flimsy and transitory like they were now.

The ground floor was obscured by a garden trellis, some sort of evergreen climbing plant coiled its tendrils way through the latticing. The top floor was dominated by a large bay window.

It took a couple of minutes for Hamson and Fowler to arrive. When they did, Gray was already out of the car and leaning on it.

"Are you sure you want to do this? You knew her, after all."

Once Gray had finally composed himself, Tanya's cause of death had been clear to see. Shot in the back and the back of her head bashed in. Either one would probably have killed her. So far, no gun had been found in the vicinity. The image was still bright in his mind.

"We're wasting time," he said.

Allowing Hamson no further pause for thought he led the pair into the small garden which, in the wall's shadow, was relatively bare, shrubs and plants cut back for winter like David Hill's plot at the vicarage. Empty window boxes clung to the sills of the downstairs bay window and equally bereft baskets dangled either side of a carefully painted blue front door. The plot smacked of preparation and attention in equal measures.

There was a porch of sorts under which a young constable sheltered, shivering with the cold, visibly uncomfortable with his lot. A wreath hung on the door, once celebrating Christmas, now commiserating loss.

A flash of Gray's warrant card brought a salute from the PC. He shifted sideways to allow them access, knocking into a hanging basket in the process.

"Shit," he said, then remembered himself. "Sorry, Ma'am."

"It's not her you should be apologising to," said Fowler. "Swearing is against my religion."

"Sorry, sir."

"Don't do it again."

"You're such an idiot, Fowler," said Hamson.

"I know. Lead on, MacDuff."

"MacDuff was a man."

"I can't know everything, can I?"

"Knowing something would be a start."

The constable watched the exchange with curiosity. It must have been the most interesting thing he'd seen all day. Gray arched an eyebrow at him. The constable lurched back into attentiveness and unlocked the door for them.

"Well, this place is rather twee," said Fowler.

Ignoring Fowler, Gray peered down the exposed hallway. A long pew and boxes of hats and gloves underneath, a coat rack above and bookshelves further along.

The arrangement gave the narrow corridor a tighter, homely feel. It was as if Tanya had moved from a large to a small house and possessed neither the space for everything nor the heart to declutter.

The walls might have been painted white, although it was hard to tell because nearly every inch was obscured by photographs and mirrors of different shapes and sizes. Gray scrutinised one of the pictures. Two young boys in dated clothing.

"Presumably her kids," said Hamson. "Next of kin will have to be informed."

"She's a looker." Fowler pointed at a picture of Tanya in front of the pyramids.

"She's dead," said Gray, "have some respect."

Gray caught Fowler pulling a face at Hamson. He bit back another rebuke and instead stepped into the reception room on the left. Unlike his, the living and dining space had been combined. He decided that any similarity between their houses was merely circumspect. Tanya's had a much warmer feel, much more lived-in. It was a home. There was a good feeling here, the type of atmosphere interior designers fell over themselves to create.

The kitchen was also unlike Gray's. Wide, spacious, well-lit and professional-looking equipment on the surfaces. There was a breakfast bar and a small table with a couple of chairs adjacent to some French windows.

Gray randomly opened cupboards. Well-stocked with provisions, but they held nothing of interest. Not that he knew what he was looking for.

From the selection of carefully arranged paraphernalia on its own shelf, Tanya was obviously a woman who'd appreciated her coffee. But then he'd known that from the way she'd made his. Past tense – Gray was already thinking about Tanya as history.

"Nice garden," said Hamson, interrupting his melancholy. She peered out of the French windows which allowed access onto a well-tended lawn bordered by mature shrubs, themselves bounded by high, flint-encrusted walls.

Upstairs, a double bedroom at the back overlooked the garden, and there were a couple of smaller rooms with made-up beds, presumably for her kids when they came home, as well as a bathroom which positively sparkled.

After a cursory inspection Gray returned to the master bedroom. He sat down on the mattress, which gave easily under his weight.

His fingers found the bottle of pills in his pocket. A brief shake and one dropped into his palm. It would help him feel numb.

CAFÉ TANYA WAS NEXT.

"Not the best of names, is it?" said Fowler.

"Shut up, Mike," said Hamson. She threw a look at Gray which he felt and ignored, just like he'd ignored her repeated suggestion to take a break.

He ignored it all. The pill had kicked in and Gray was starting to feel numb, Fowler's barbs barely piercing his skin.

"May I?" asked Gray.

Hamson acquiesced with a single, brief nod. He stepped inside, forced himself to scan the café interior that was so familiar, and yet now so alien. The low, mid-afternoon sun shone brightly through the plate glass windows. He went behind the counter, which gave him a different perspective on the space.

The display unit was empty. Presumably the food was transferred to a fridge each night. He reached out to the coffee machine. It was cold.

Next was the kitchen area. He'd seen Tanya exit it many times, had never given it more than a glance himself. The window blinds were down, making the room relatively dark. Fowler flicked on the light. Gray almost swore at him for ruining the atmosphere, but held his tongue.

Fowler was a spiteful bastard. He'd probably done it on purpose.

There were two rooms next to each other. One was a storage area – fridge, freezer, and cupboards. The other, which they were standing in, was the kitchen, comprising cooker, work surfaces, and a sink beneath the window. To their right was a back door.

The key was in the lock. Outside there was a small courtyard with a fence around it. An alleyway ran along one boundary. The sounds of the traffic were dully audible. It was all so depressingly normal.

Gray, unable to keep up the pretence any longer, dropped to his knees and began crying.

Thirty Eight

Gray awoke the next morning still fully clothed, face down on his living room floor. He remembered everything, knew immediately it wasn't all a dream. Tanya really was dead.

He was gripped by the mother of all hangovers. His head pounded. He wanted to throw up. He ached all over. Yet still it wasn't enough.

A steady flow of pills had helped Gray keep his emotions in check. After the café Gray had picked up some cash from his house, headed to the nearest pub, and hadn't stopped drinking until he ran out of cash, which forced him to go home. He found an old bottle of scotch in the back of a cupboard and finished it. Then nothing until this morning's close-up view of the carpet.

Tom's disappearance, Hope leaving home, Kate's suicide and funeral, they were all ultra-low points. He'd already been in the depths – each event simply sank him a little further towards Hell.

But this, in many ways, felt worse because he'd believed Tanya was maybe a path upwards. A balloon which he could hang on to and float away from the darkness.

Now she was gone too.

Two shootings in an area where murder was a once-in-a-decade occurrence. A questionable suicide. Fights, drugs, or motoring offences, yes. Not homicide.

Tanya's post-mortem was this morning. Gray checked his watch. In less than an hour. He'd have to get a move on.

A shower, a dose of painkillers large enough to fell a horse, and several espressos didn't alter how he felt.

He called Hamson. "Von, I need your help."

"Go on." She sounded wary.

"Are you attending Tanya's post-mortem?"

"Why?"

"My car's still at the station."

"Didn't you collect it yesterday?"

"And I'll need to borrow some more cash from you."

"For crying out loud!"

"Is that a yes?"

Half an hour later Gray was in Hamson's car being battered by a significant amount of sustained grumbling. It washed over him. There were far bigger issues to be bothered by than an upset boss.

Hamson's griping continued throughout the stop-start journey, as well as after she parked, paid, and hiked along the hospital corridors to the mortuary.

"Here we are again, Sergeant," said Ben Clough. He acknowledged Hamson with a nod.

Gray couldn't speak. The smell of antiseptic in the air made him feel sick.

"You're late."

"Sorry." Gray didn't know why he was apologising, or why they'd been delayed.

"The roads were a bloody nightmare," said Hamson.

"Yes, that's right." The memory bobbed to the surface of his memory. An accident at a set of traffic lights had snarled the entire grid up. Although Hamson took alternative directions it felt like everyone else was doing the same.

"I'm sorry to say I couldn't wait. We've already done Mrs Small."

Relief flooded through Gray. He hadn't really wanted to see Tanya sliced up. The lifeless expression on what had once been a vibrant face was enough to haunt his thoughts for months to come without adding further layers of horror.

"What did you find?" asked Hamson.

Clough waved a folder around. "Enter my lair and I will reveal all."

He led them down a narrow corridor and into a windowless office. The interior was a poverty of space. A desk and a couple of chairs were all that could be crammed in. Several boxes tucked against the wall gave the impression Clough had only just taken up residence.

"Would you mind shutting the door, DI Hamson? Let's have a bit of privacy."

"Of course."

Hamson couldn't comply until she'd shifted her own seat, which was the impediment. "Sorry, Sol, but could I just...?"

Gray shifted to allow Hamson room to manoeuvre.

"All done?" asked Clough sweetly.

She nodded. Gray settled down into an uncomfortable seat that had seen far better days. He placed his arms on the rests and tried to relax, found himself gripping the wood.

Clough opened the report and glanced down. It was simply for effect. From past experience, Gray knew that the pathologist would be thoroughly familiar with the contents.

"The victim was killed by a single gunshot from behind, which pierced the heart. Death would have been pretty much instantaneous," said Clough. "The wound was a straight in-and-out. Gunpowder residue around the entrance wound, but no abrasion ring."

"So the calibre of weapon could be the same in both murders?" asked Gray.

"Ballistics will confirm," said Hamson. She turned to Gray. "We brought in a metal detectorist to probe the beach, one of those hobby guys. They found the slug pretty quickly." This was news to him.

"Then there was the head trauma. A single strike by a blunt, misshapen object, possibly a rock. I found some stone chips within the wound. It's difficult to tell whether the impact occurred just before or after she was shot."

"How so?"

"She could have struck her head when she collapsed."

"The body was found on sand, nowhere near anything that could cause that kind of damage."

"Maybe the incoming tide picked her up, moved her around?"

"Possibly. Or she was hit first."

"The stomach contained a partially digested last meal, a curry by appearance and odour, although not in a great quantity. In comparison, her blood alcohol level was very high. There were also signs of a recent sexual activity."

"How recent?"

Gray was surprised his expression didn't give him away. Roiling within was a toxic cocktail. Of loss and guilt. He still felt like spilling his guts on Clough's desk, confessing all, and being dragged away to prison for the rest of his life.

He stayed mute.

"Certainly less than a day," said Clough. "Maybe even within a few hours of her death. No semen deposit though."

"Condom?"

"Impossible to tell after her immersion in the brine."

"Maybe she went for a walk on the beach to bask in the afterglow and somebody killed her."

"Poetically put, Inspector. I took the liberty of combing her pubic region and found some hairs that clearly weren't hers. I'd assume from her sexual partner. I've sent them away for analysis. It'll be a couple of days before I get anything back from the lab.

"Other than that she was relatively fit, in possession of very little excess fat, healthy heart and lungs too. Theoretically, Mrs Small had plenty of enjoyable years ahead of her."

"Thanks, Doctor."

They took their leave.

Gray ran a hand over his face. Tanya. Who would want to kill Tanya?

"Want to talk about it?"

"Not really."

"Your call. And don't worry about the outburst, I never forget."

Trawling after Hamson, Gray was irritated with himself. Hamson unlocked the car and they climbed in. She was driving.

Gray stared out the window in a silence which Hamson, eventually, couldn't help breaking. "Did you know her very well?"

He thought about that one. He and Tanya had talked most days for the last few weeks, had sex once. He played it safe and just on the wrong side of accurate. "I bought coffee from her every morning."

"Well, you'll have to go somewhere else from now on."

Gray didn't have a reply to that.

Thirty Nine

B ack at the station, Gray headed straight to the incident room and the whiteboard. Buckingham's notes were still on the board, though there hadn't been any recent information to add. The office hadn't seen this much action in years. Buckingham, Hill, and Tanya fought for space in his tired mind.

There was plenty to read about Tanya – a mass of neat notes and a wealth of photographs, all but one of them displaying his one-night stand in death. It was hard to take. He needed some space, to be away from the hurly-burly of the murder investigation.

From the corner of his eye Gray watched Hamson enter one of the meeting rooms and engage in an animated conversation with Carslake. Which left only Fowler to talk to.

"I don't see anything up there about CCTV, Mike. Is a review underway?"

"We've only just finished checking the footage." Fowler was surly.

"And?"

Fowler shrugged. "Just Mrs Small walking down the High Street and along the cliff top until she descended onto the beach via the steps at Viking Bay."

"Alone?"

"Nobody suspicious. It's Broadstairs, not Margate. I'll go down to the pubs and restaurants on the jetty, see if they've any cameras. We may catch a break there."

Gray didn't bother to thank Fowler and retreated to his desk. Ten minutes later Hamson appeared in his blurred peripheral vision. He kept his eyes forward. "What is it Von? I'm busy."

"How are you feeling?"

"Bloody awful."

"Good. You deserve it."

"Thanks."

"You're a fucking idiot." Her words were lava spilling out from her lips.

"What?"

"There's a bloke come into the station with something to say that might interest you."

"I seriously doubt it."

"Believe me, you'll be interested. Get your arse along to interview room three."

HAMSON REFUSED TO UTTER another word. She walked as if trying to stab her heels through the lino floor. The sound chipped away at Gray's temples. She didn't even hold the door into the interview room for him. A man fixed a glare on them as they entered.

"About bloody time," he said.

"Apologies for the delay, Mr Philips."

Philips, remained seated, a mug on the table before him. He wore a well-pressed white shirt and a black tie. He was clean shaven, and his thinning hair was neatly combed. Gray held his hand out. Philips shook it. His grip was firm and dry. Gray drooped into a chair. Hamson followed suit in a more angular fashion. She crossed her legs, sat back a short distance, just out of Gray's line of sight.

"You'll excuse me if I don't stand," said Philips. "I'm knackered. Only just finished my shift."

"I can sympathise," said Hamson.

"Night's the best time to be a taxi driver, though. Good money to be made. Why am I still here? I really need to get some sleep."

"I'd like you to repeat what you told me for my colleague's benefit."

Gray noted Hamson hadn't bothered to introduce him. He was too foggy to think about it properly, assumed she was just angry.

"All of it?" asked Philips.

A nod from Hamson drew a sigh from the taxi driver. "And then I can go?" Another nod, a further exhalation. "It's about the woman on the beach. As soon as I saw her photo in the newspaper I knew straight away."

"What about her?"

"The night she died I was working in Margate. I always pull the late shift."

"Popular with the wife," said Gray.

"Not really," said Philips, Gray's poor attempt at humour falling flat. "It doesn't matter anymore. She left."

"I'm sorry to hear that."

"Don't be. Best thing that ever happened to me. No mortgage, no kids, nothing."

"Go on, Mr Philips," said Hamson. "The sooner you tell us, the sooner you can go."

"You're right. Where was I?"

"Margate."

Philips clicked his fingers in recollection. "The dead woman got into my taxi. Before she was dead, of course. I took her to Broadstairs."

A fist reached into Gray's gut and twisted.

"Do you recall the address?"

"I've picked up a lot of people since then. It was somewhere at the top end of town."

"Not near the beach?"

Philips shook his head. "And she wasn't alone. She was with a man. They were together, if you know what I mean. Romantically involved."

"What did he look like?"

"I didn't see him, only her. She did all the talking and it was dark. She even paid. What a gentleman her other half was!"

Gray began to relax. Maybe he'd get through this.

"He left something behind, though."

"This?" Hamson held something up.

"Yes."

A battered black wallet, clad in a clear plastic evidence bag, hit the table. Gray's world shrunk to that single piece of well-worn leather.

She stood, the chair legs scraping, said, "Thanks for coming in, Mr Philips."

"Is that it?"

"Unless you've anything else to add?"

The taxi driver shook his head.

"I'll show you out."

"My information is important, right?"

"Yes."

"I hope you catch the bastard."

Hamson picked up the wallet before escorting him out. When she returned, Hamson towered over Gray like one of the gravestones in the St Peters churchyard.

"I know why you called me an idiot now," he said.

"About time you applied some intelligence to all this."

"Sorry."

"Sorry? That's it?"

"What else do you want me to say?"

"You were Tanya's sexual partner, right?"

"It's not what you think..."

Hamson reared up. "Don't go making excuses! For once tell me the fucking truth!"

"It was just once."

"What's the frequency got to do with it? You and Tanya were together immediately before her death, yes?"

Gray nodded, his head heavy, skull threatening to split apart.

"My God. And you didn't say anything." Hamson put her head in her hands. "Can you comprehend what you've done? How much you've exposed both of us?"

Gray couldn't speak.

"This could be the end of both our careers," said Hamson. "You fucking fool."

"You'll be fine. You didn't know about any of it."

"I'm your commanding officer, Sol! The buck stops with me. Can't you see that?"

Gray couldn't answer.

"And the DCI isn't my biggest fan in the first place." She flopped into a sitting position, stared at Gray with resignation.

"I saw you two chatting."

"It was more of a one-way bollocking."

Before Gray could reply there was a knock on the door, and it opened. In stepped Carslake.

"I'll take over from here, Yvonne."

"Yes, Sir." Hamson stood up and left the room. Carslake took her seat. For a few moments Carslake and Gray eyed each other.

"You're a bloody fool," said Carslake eventually.

"I know. And I'm aware I can't be part of the investigation anymore."

"That's big of you. Actually, you can't be part of anything because you're being suspended, pending an enquiry." Carslake shook his head. "Frankly you're lucky it's just a suspension. It's only because of our friendship you're being allowed to go home and not going straight into a cell."

Gray opened his mouth to thank Carslake but the DCI raised a hand and interrupted him. "I don't want to hear it."

"I'll get my coat."

"There's one job to do before you go home."

GRAY DROVE SLOWLY TO the hospital. He suspected that if he was stopped en route he'd be over the limit. Thankfully there weren't many cops around here. He should know. His head was pounding, as much with Philips' revelation as the after-effects of last night.

Luckily, he made it to his destination without incident, found a parking spot, and left the car at a haphazard angle. He didn't bother paying the parking charge. A fine was the least of his worries.

Clough was in his tiny office, tapping away at a keyboard. When his eyes alighted on Gray an expression of intrigue surfaced. Wordlessly, the pathologist handed over a sample jar. He permitted a moment's privacy by stepping into the corridor while Gray extracted several pubes and slotted them into the screw-top container. The pathologist couldn't meet Gray's eyes when he took back the evidence.

Forty

The first thing Gray did when he got home was to swallow another of Mallory's pills. He paused to luxuriate in the ensuing numbness delivered by the little white pill before he attempted the second task. A call to his bank, cancelling his credit cards, all of which were in his confiscated wallet. Next, he arranged the collection of some emergency cash from over the counter because his money was in the same place as the cards.

Then he went out to get drunk again.

GRAY WAS STEADILY ACHIEVING his objective of attaining oblivion when trouble came for him in a corner of The Tartar Frigate, a pub on the Broadstairs seafront.

The first sign of Gray's impending doom was an intruding voice that he immediately recognised. "Solomon Gray."

He turned.

Scully.

The reporter pushed with his mouth again, unhappy Gray was ignoring him. "Hey, I'm talking to you."

"Fuck off," said Gray.

"You're such a pompous prick."

"Whatever. Leave me alone." Gray went back to his pint. Took a swig of the beer, his fingers tight around the glass.

"I was right. Tell me I was right," said Scully. He empha-
sised his words by shoving Gray's shoulder. Beer spilled across
the table.

Gray stared at the pool spreading across the dark varnished
wood. Slowly, he twisted his head over a tense shoulder. The
reporter was leering at him, a shit-eating grin plastered across
his repugnant face. A couple of Scully's colleagues in the background at the bar were enjoying the spectacle. The pub had fall-
en silent, waiting to see what would occur.

Scully shoved him again. Something clicked out of place
inside Gray, fracturing his self-control.

The next thing Gray knew, he was standing over a prostrate
Scully, trying to put a boot into his ribs. The reporter's col-
leagues were holding him, meaning Gray couldn't quite reach.
His knuckles throbbed. They were skinned, raw.

Shocked faces. Silence.

Then someone shouted, "Call the police."

"I am the police," said Gray. "I told him. I told Scully the
next time we met I'd stick a fist in his face. He asked for it." He
shook off the journalists. "You're all witnesses." Gray moved a
finger in a semi-circle to encompass everyone.

Within seconds he was outside in the open air. He glanced
in through the window. A dazed Scully was being pulled to his
feet. He decided it would be prudent to withdraw before they
came looking for him.

GRAY UNLOCKED HIS DOOR and fell into the hallway.
It was well into the evening and Gray couldn't see a thing. He
felt for the light switch. As his fingers touched it he changed

his mind. So he stayed in the dark and fumbled his way along the corridor, the weight of the beers he was carrying altering his already off-kilter centre of gravity.

He staggered down the two steps into the kitchen. The alcohol made him forget they were there, despite him negotiating them for the best part of twenty years. The beers almost ended up on the floor when he mistakenly estimated the kitchen unit he was aiming for to be wider than it actually was. He fished around for a bottle, snagged one.

Given his condition, there was no way Gray would be able to pop the cap in the dark. He started the torch app on his phone. The bright beam cut through the darkness.

"Ouch." Gray squinted against the glare.

The drawer opened with a rattle. He shushed it into silence, seized the bottle opener, levered open the Bishop's Finger, a powerful local Kentish brew. At a couple of per cent alcohol higher than your average bitter it was the sort of booze to start the night, not close it.

At the third attempt he succeeded. A hiss, and foam poured out of the neck. Gray raised the bottle to his mouth and sipped it away.

Bugger the glass.

He took the bottle into the dark living room and sank into a soft armchair. Like the television that stood in the corner, the seat was hardly used and still smelled new even though it wasn't. He drained the first beer quickly. A moment later he returned with the bag and the opener, purely for efficiency's sake.

Halfway through his third there was a tentative knock at the front door. Gray ignored it and the successive heavier thumping.

The letter box fluttered. "I know you're in there."

"Go away, Yvonne! And tell Carslake to bugger off while you're at it."

"The DCI doesn't know I'm here."

"Good for you. The answer's the same."

The flap snapped shut. Gray smirked with success. As he was lifting the bottle to toast Hamson's departure the living room light flicked on. He grimaced in the harsh white beam. Standing in the doorway was the DI herself.

"Turn that bloody thing off!"

Hamson complied.

"I can't see," she said.

His fingers fumbled until they closed on a lamp switch. The resulting illumination was soft.

"Thanks," said Hamson.

"How did you get in?"

"You left these in the lock." Hamson held up a bunch of keys.

"I didn't even know I'd mislaid them."

"Good job it was me who found them." Gray was too drunk to care. She dropped the keys onto a side table.

"Take a seat. And have a beer." Gray pointed at the bag which was obscured by the armchair.

"No thanks, I'm at least a week away from facing another drop of alcohol."

"It wasn't an invitation." With a practiced flourish that belied his hammered state, Gray popped the cap and passed one to Hamson.

"Got a glass?"

"Nope, all smashed."

Accepting the bullshit at face value Hamson said, "Looks like it's a bottle, then. What happened to your knuckles?"

Gray twisted his hand, remembered the blood flowing from Scully's gums. "I fell over."

"Right." Hamson wiped the neck of her bottle, took a drink, and grimaced.

"You should see your face."

"You should see yours. You look like a drunk."

"I am a drunk. Tonight at least. Why are you here? Last I knew you were stabbing me in the back."

"That's harsh, Sol."

"It's a fact."

"I'm checking on you, obviously. Although I wonder why now. I didn't enjoy suspending you."

"How sweet." Gray couldn't help but load his comment with sarcasm. "And totally unnecessary. Now you've seen I'm a mess you can leave me to it. Come tomorrow morning, I'll be back to my old self. In fact, I'm going to take my beer to bed."

Gray tried to stand, failed, and fell back down, missing the chair entirely and landing heavily on his backside. "Perhaps I'll sleep here tonight."

"I'll give you a hand."

"I'm not an invalid."

"You're pissed."

"That's an irrefutable charge."

Taking one of Gray's hands she pulled him upright. Something fell out of Gray's pocket. Hamson bent to pick it up.

"Why do you have a photo of Buckingham?"

"Because he's the same age as Tom. It's a reminder."

"Come on, let's get you upstairs."

He leaned on Hamson, who wasn't much shorter than a slumped Gray, and a damn sight stronger than she looked. The stairs were a mountain and they took each step slowly, Gray adopting the banister as additional support. On the first floor he said, "Just leave me in one of the bedrooms."

The DI headed to the nearest door and flicked the switch. The room was bereft of furniture.

"Here'll be fine," said Gray.

"You'll freeze."

"I'll sleep in my clothes."

"Not a chance." She turned the light off.

The next door was locked. Hamson rattled the handle. It wouldn't budge. She frowned. Hamson wasn't to know it used to be the master bedroom. No one had entered since Kate's body had been carted out.

"We're going further up," said Hamson.

On the top flight was a single door. The roof sloped left and right of the landing. "No lights," he said and went inside.

He sagged onto the bed and heard Hamson beside him, felt covers slide up over his body. The fingers of sleep began to creep over him.

"I think I just stepped on something," she said.

"That's private, leave it."

She ignored Gray's demand and lit the cramped confines via the bedside lamp.

"What's all this stuff, Sol?" She pointed to one of the piles of paper that made the small space seemed cramped.

"Private, I told you."

Hamson picked up a folder. Through blurry eyes Gray read the sticker on the outside: "Nick Buckingham." She glanced inside, then looked at Gray, her mouth hanging open. "These are official police documents."

She began lifting files and folders, flicking through them. "They're all related to Tom."

"Of course. Did you think I'd ever stop looking for him?"

"I know, but this?" Hamson indicated the mounds of paperwork with a sweeping arm. "There's *years* of information here."

"He's been gone years, Von."

Hamson stood in the centre of what little unoccupied floor space there was. "I don't know what to do about this, Sol, I really don't. Having all these files illegally is hardly going to help your case."

Gray wasn't bothered that she'd found out. It felt like a relief, something he'd suppressed for such a long time, now released. Perhaps this would help his fragile mental state. Or maybe this was all the beer talking. He'd know for sure in the morning.

"Do what you must, Ma'am." Rolling over, Gray flicked the lamp off and pulled the duvet up to his chin.

"I'll be back tomorrow," she said.

Heels clattered down the stairs. Even they sounded fed up with Gray.

Forty One

Five Years Ago

Gray had a bottle in his hand. He wasn't sure what it was. Vodka maybe? He wasn't sure what time it was either. He'd left Kate's wake hours ago, slipped out when nobody was looking, turned his phone off, caught a bus back to Broadstairs, and carried on drinking.

They threw Gray out of the pub when he started crying again. More accurately, when he couldn't stop crying. Great gouts of loss welling up inside him that needed to be released.

He had no recollection of making it home, unlocking the door, picking up the booze. His first memory was of standing in the room. He stared at their bed. Where Kate had passed on. By her own hand. Gray flopped onto the floor and cried till he was dry.

Then he was next door in the bathroom. His reflection stared back at him in the mirror. So low he couldn't possibly fall any further. Ragged, unkempt, lifeless eyes.

Behind the mirror was a medicine cabinet. Full of over-the-counter pills and drugs. They made a twisted sense to Gray. He grabbed a handful of bottles. He needed to lie down. The nearest space was the bath. He clambered into it fully clothed. The pill bottles were arranged along the wall, the vodka bottle stayed in his grasp, which he drank from regularly.

The pills were a way to escape all the pain. He could do it. He could swallow them down and that would be the end.

Instead, Gray had another drink.

HE WAS SHAKING VIOLENTLY, agitated by some unseen hand. Gray opened his eyes, saw Carslake and David Hill leaning over him, Alice in the background, expressions of fear on all their faces.

"Thank God!" said David.

"We thought you'd ended it," said Carslake. He was holding the half-empty vodka bottle. "Did you take anything?"

Gray realised he must have fallen asleep. He couldn't remember whether he'd taken any pills or not. They were spread all around him in the bath, various shapes and colours. Gray said he didn't know.

"I'll call an ambulance," said Alice.

Gray's protests fell on deaf ears. The paramedics arrived. Gray was subjected to several rapid examinations. A fast drive to the hospital and Gray had his stomach pumped before unconsciousness took hold again. The last thing he remembered was Carslake promising that Gray would get help.

But Gray didn't want any.

Forty Two

The smell of coffee filled the kitchen. Vibrant and earthy, it reminded Gray of somewhere else, another time, when children chased each other round the room before breakfast, and Kate chided them that their pancakes were getting cold. But that time was long gone. Because he was here now. On the brink of unemployment. Alone. Adrift. Abandoned.

They were bound to be here soon. Until then, Gray drank coffee, smoked, and regarded his garden, which was as tangled and chaotic as his life.

The doorbell chimed. It was time and it was Hamson. She wasn't alone. Two uniforms flanked her, looking stern.

"Get dressed, Sol. I need you to answer some questions down at the station."

Gray turned away and left the door open for Hamson while he went upstairs to throw some clothes on and take a pill. Maybe his last for a while.

"TELL ME ABOUT YESTERDAY," said Hamson. They sat in interview room three again, Gray where Philips had sat, Hamson opposite. In a surprising move, Pennance was riding shotgun. Engaging an outsider. Where was Carslake?

It had been well over an hour since they'd brought him in, and it was formal. Every noise was being recorded. Just like the interrogation after Tom's disappearance.

"Which bit? It was a long day."

"Between me suspending you and going to your house."

Pennance pitched a glance at Hamson, which she ignored.

"I went out for a drink," said Gray.

"More than one?"

"It's not become illegal in the last twenty-four hours, has it?"

Ignoring the sarcasm Hamson asked, "Where?"

Gray reeled off the five pubs he'd patronised. The Tartar Frigate was the concluding stop.

"Tell me about your knuckles."

"I scuffed them."

"On what?"

"Someone who deserved it."

"Witnesses say the 'who' was Ed Scully."

"I won't deny it. I warned him."

"And then what happened?"

"I went home. You know I did."

"Do I?"

"You saw me."

"There's a half-hour gap between you knocking out Scully and me finding your keys in your door. What happened in between?"

"Stared at the sea for a bit. Walked home. Went to the off-licence."

"Which one?"

"The Bottleneck."

"We'll check the CCTV."

"What's all this about?"

Her response was the heavy descent of paperwork onto the table. "Talk to me about that."

Gray didn't immediately recognise the inch-thick stack of papers in front of him. Then the sun pushed through the clouds in his brain. "You've been back to my house."

"A judge granted a warrant this morning. It took three men half an hour to bag everything up."

From a buff folder Hamson produced another piece of evidence. It was the photo of Buckingham he'd been keeping.

"And this one?"

"A reminder of the boy. No one else seems to care about him."

"That's not strictly correct, Sol," said Pennance.

"He's just evidence to you," said Gray. "Nothing more. Why am I here, Von?"

"It's Detective Inspector Hamson. And you had sex with Tanya Small immediately before she was murdered, then kept it to yourself. That's sufficient in itself."

He couldn't deny it.

"How did you get the case notes?"

Gray unburdened himself with the energy of someone who'd been holding up a weight for far too long. "I made copies. At night, when no one was around. Over the months and years. Anything related to Tom, no matter how slight. I never stopped trying to find him."

"Touching," said Pennance. He'd been unusually quiet so far.

"What are you even doing here?" Gray stabbed a finger at him.

"DI Pennance asked to be involved. I thought it a good suggestion."

"Have you taken leave of your senses, Von?"

"I'm not the one sitting on that side of the table."

Gray didn't have an answer. He crossed his arms, shifted his chair slightly so he wasn't directly facing Pennance.

Hamson brought the conversation back on track. "It's against regulations to have official police documentation in your possession."

"Tell me something I don't know."

She said nothing at first, rattled her fingers on the table. Hamson flipped open the folder, turned it so it faced Gray. Inside was the photo of Buckingham and his unseen sexual partner, which Gray had received anonymously by email.

"It wasn't very well hidden," said Hamson.

"I wasn't planning on having my house burgled."

"We followed due process. This is evidence."

"Why arrest me now? Search my house?"

"It's Ed Scully," said Hamson eventually.

"Is he pressing charges?"

"He's dead."

Gray shifted forward in his seat. "What? How?"

The documents went, Hamson replacing them with a photo of the man himself. Scully was seated in what looked to be a living room, open-mouthed in apparent shock, a huge hole in his chest. Gray had seen enough corpses to recognise the cause of death. His head spun.

"Someone shot him," confirmed Hamson. "Know anything about it?"

"Why should I?"

"Would it be fair to say you hated Scully?"

"I loathed the man and the feeling was mutual."

"Do you care that he's dead?"

"The world's a better place without him. But it wasn't me who shot him. I wouldn't go to prison for that man."

Hamson regarded Gray for a long moment. "Three murders in a town where homicide is a rarity. We've been looking for something that connects these deaths, besides the weapon. Now I think I know what that something is."

"Enlighten me."

"You. You knew them all," said Hamson. "In fact, it would appear that you knew Tanya Small...*intimately*. In her case, you were the last person to see her alive and you've already admitted to hating Scully."

"Is this some sort of sick joke? You know I didn't kill them."

"This isn't going anywhere," said Pennance.

"I agree," said Hamson. She seemed grimly determined. "Solomon Gray, I'm arresting you for the murders of Tanya Small and Edward Scully..."

Gray didn't hear the rest of his rights being read, nor did he resist when he was led away to be processed.

His fingers were swabbed for gunpowder residue. He was put into a cell where he would spend the night. The clang of the door shutting barely troubled his ear drums. The hard surface of the bench didn't register with his nerve endings as he sat down.

Gray held his hands out before him, wondered what they'd done. Was it true? Had he killed Scully?

Was he, Solomon Gray, a murderer?

Forty Three

Over the following forty-eight hours Gray was moved from lockup to interview room a further five times.

The first occasion followed soon after his processing and was necessarily fleeting. He was offered representation. Gray refused.

The second was the following day. He'd barely slept, surrounded by familiar yet alien sounds and a routine that wasn't his. Hamson and Pennance were seated when Gray was brought in. Hamson gave Gray a hard look as he sat down. He was too tired to respond.

"How long had you and Mrs Small been in a relationship?" said Hamson.

"It was hardly a relationship. I spoke to her most days at the café, but the conversation was confined to food and drink orders. We only got to know each other properly over recent weeks."

"How did you feel when you saw Mrs Small dead on the beach?"

"Shocked, of course."

"Why didn't you say anything at the time about having slept with Mrs Small or afterwards? You had plenty of opportunity to do so."

"I don't know. It became more difficult to tell you the longer it went on."

"Because it made you look guilty?"

"I didn't kill her."

"Do you own a gun?"

"No."

"You'd know where to get one from. Frank McGavin, for example."

"That's ridiculous."

"I'm wondering if that's why you delayed making mention about Mrs Small and you? To give you time to wash away the gun residue, to cover your tracks?"

"No."

"And she was found in an area where CCTV was non-existent. I think you took her there and killed her."

"Why would I do that?"

"That's what I'm trying to find out."

Gray leaned over the table. "I'm as keen as you are to find out what happened to Tanya. I liked her. A lot. I didn't kill her." Point made, Gray sat upright again.

"And what about these?"

Hamson placed a pill bottle on the table. Gray itched to snatch the container, to place a tablet on the tip of his tongue. He kept his hands pressed between his legs, out of sight. He hoped the twitching wasn't visible.

"Your records show Occupational Health referred you for an examination recently," she said. "Care to explain, Sol?"

"Talk to my doctor."

"Mallory? I have. He cited patient confidentiality when I called him. We'd need your consent for him to release the information."

"Which I'm not giving you."

"Which is okay, because the Internet's a wonderful thing," she said, holding the bottle so the label faced Gray. "I searched for the brand name on the label. These are for depression."

"The doctor prescribed them. Who am I to argue?"

"You should have said."

"I'm under no obligation to tell you or anyone else anything. Besides, Carslake knew everything. In fact, he ordered me to visit Mallory."

"That's not how the DCI sees it."

Gray looked from Hamson to Pennance. The realisation struck him like a freight train. It explained why he'd seen nothing of Carslake.

"So that's how it's going to be?" he said.

"Looks like the old boys' club isn't such a friendly place, after all."

"I've nothing else to say."

"That won't help you."

"You're right, I'll get that lawyer now."

"Is there anyone you'd like?"

"The duty solicitor will do."

Hamson nodded and ended the interview.

Two further interviews over the rest of the day brought more questions about Tanya and Scully. Hamson kept hammering away, Pennance sitting back, seeing all and saying nothing, the duty solicitor interjecting periodically. Gray kept repeating that he had nothing more to say until Hamson gave up and had him returned to the cell for the night.

The next morning Morgan unlocked the cell door. Gray groaned and stood up. He'd slept poorly again and eaten very little of his breakfast.

When he entered the interview room with his solicitor there was a change. No Pennance. In his place was Carslake, Hamson by his side in the subordinate role. Time was reaching the point where either they had to make the charge stick, or release him.

"How are you, DS Gray?" Carslake, elbows on the table, leaned over, a déjà vu of sorts from ten years prior. Carslake interviewing Gray once again.

Gray wasn't about to reveal anything. "Stupendous, sir."

"I'm glad to hear it."

"Are you?"

"Of course."

"Where have you been? Where were you when I needed you?"

Carslake's expression hardened while Hamson shrunk in on herself.

"The charges against you are very serious."

"I don't mean now. For the last decade you've gradually pulled away, Jeff. You've let me drift."

"These charges follow on from mental health issues and an accusation of rape."

"The rape accusation was recanted and has no bearing on the current allegations," said Gray's solicitor.

Carslake nodded to accept the point.

"What mental health issues?" asked Hamson.

It was as if the two of them were holding separate conversations.

"Where were you?" shouted Gray. He slammed his fist onto the table top.

Carslake face reddened, the only outward response to Gray's question. "Due process has to be carried out."

"Like last time? When Tom disappeared?"

"That was different!" snapped Carslake. "We were on the same side."

"What about now, Jeff?"

"Due process has to be followed," repeated Carslake.

"You were my friend!"

Carslake blinked. He quietly said, "I still am."

"Not from where I'm sitting. On the wrong side of the table."

"Due process—"

"I know!" interrupted Gray. "It has to be followed. Change the record."

"Chief Inspector," said Gray's solicitor, "either charge my client or let him go."

"Detective Sergeant Gray, we are releasing you on bail, pending further investigation. Regardless of the outcome there will be a formal enquiry into your conduct," said Carslake and pushed himself upright. "Please show DS Gray out, DI Hamson, then come up to my office." The door banged behind Carslake.

"Getting time with the DCI after all, Von? I told you to be careful what you wished for."

Hamson ignored the jibe. "You've really let me down, Sol. If you'd just been straight with me on the beach, we could have avoided most of this."

She stood and held the door open for Gray and his solicitor. She wouldn't meet his eye.

Hamson signed Gray out, handing back his personal belongings. She led him to the front desk.

"Do I get a lift?" Gray asked.

"No," said Hamson said and walked away.

"Bye, then."

Gray stepped outside. He didn't have anyone to call and not enough cash in his pocket for a taxi. It was the bus, then.

It started to rain as he walked to the nearest stop. The cold water on Gray's face brought with it some clarity. What Hamson had said about the CCTV dropped into place. He needed to speak to her, but couldn't go back to the station. It would look wrong. And they'd taken his work mobile.

So Gray had to wait until he reached home, all the while his suspicions growing.

Forty Four

As soon as Gray got home he sank a large measure of whisky for medicinal purposes. He poured a second drink and carried it up to the bathroom. He took a hot shower in an effort to tackle the rawness at the back of his throat which promised the mother of all colds.

He'd been soaked to the skin while he waited for the bus. No shelter to hide under. His transport, when it finally arrived, was slow. The bus took a circuitous route between Margate, Ramsgate, and Broadstairs and he'd observed most of the three towns at a snail's pace through rain-speckled glass.

In pyjamas and dressing gown he surveyed the damage wrought by the investigating officers. It wasn't too bad considering, although his attic room was the emptiest he'd seen it in a decade. They'd taken every last scrap of paper.

THE KNOCK CAME WHEN Gray was heading downstairs for another drink. Hamson was on the step. Downcast, yet defiant. The rain was still lashing down.

"I know, you were just doing your job," he said.

"Doing Carslake's."

Gray left Hamson there and went through to the kitchen, opened a cupboard, groped for what he wanted. The door slammed shut and Gray felt her presence beside him.

"Want one?" Gray waved the whisky bottle at Hamson.

"Can I get a shot in a coffee?"

"It's malt, you heathen."

"I need caffeine and booze."

"As it's you." The kettle went on the hob. While the water heated, he leaned on the work surface and crossed his arms. "Well?"

"Yes, I've got it." Hamson showed him a USB stick.

"Laptop?" A shift of her shoulder showed Gray the bag hanging. "Seeing as mine's yet to be returned."

"Care to tell me what's going on?"

"When I'm a little further down the path of righteousness."

"What?"

"My little joke."

He watched Hamson while he made the drinks. She smoked two cigarettes in quick succession huddled beneath an umbrella. She'd refused the option to stay inside. It seemed to be her way of being clean about a dirty habit. He realised that her presence at his house meant Hamson was about as far away from everyone else as she could get.

"I'll swap you," he said, held out the mug of alcohol-laced coffee. She took a deep swallow, careless of the liquid's temperature, holding out the cigarette packet with the other hand, exposing herself to the rain.

"What about you?" she asked.

Gray extracted the whisky bottle from his pocket. Hamson managed a weak smile.

"You're getting wet," she said. "Get underneath the brolly."

They stood shoulder to shoulder. She drew on her cigarette. Gray smelled menthol. A check on the front of the packet confirmed his suspicion. He hated them. It was like having a cough sweet. Despite deep reservations he popped the cigarette between his lips and handed the rest back. He patted his pockets. "Got a light?"

A brief kiss of the ember. "Thanks."

"Don't mention it," said Hamson. She lit another cigarette and dropped the dead end onto the grass. "Sorry, I'll pick them up before I go."

"Because it's so tidy otherwise." He waved an expansive arm at the surrounding jungle.

"I'm also sorry about what you had to go through. I sat outside in the car for ten minutes before I could bring myself to knock."

"We're friends." And he needed all the friends he could get. Carslake no longer fit the description. Now that he thought about it, Carslake hadn't been a friend in a long time. Gray just hadn't been able to admit it. "What did Carslake say?"

"I haven't been up to see him yet."

"Ignoring a direct order, Von? Whatever next?"

"A major bollocking, for sure."

Gray didn't try to console Hamson. They both would've seen it for the lie it was.

"You'd better get back," he said. "Get it over with."

"I know, just not yet though." Hamson raised her coffee. "Dutch courage."

HAMSON CLIMBED INTO her car and slowly drove away. As soon as she was out of sight Gray shifted away from the curtain, headed back into the kitchen and fired up the laptop. He tilted the computer, looking for a USB port, then plugged in the flash drive.

In seconds a new window popped up, a folder containing one file. Gray put his finger on the mouse pad and awkwardly shunted the arrow over the file. He clicked twice to open. The file was a video clip, a montage of grainy CCTV camera footage following his stagger through Broadstairs. About thirty seconds in he saw himself stop and strike up a conversation with a familiar person.

This was it.

Forty Five

She was seated, as always, on her pew in St Peter's Church. Gray slipped in next to her.

"Hello, Alice."

"Solomon," she said, not taking her eyes from the stained-glass window. "Pleasant to see you again." She patted the space next to her on the pew. He sat down beside her, sharing her perspective on the world.

"I know everything," he said.

"Only God knows everything."

"Why?"

"Why what?"

"Kill them all? Was it a message from God?"

"Don't be so crass, Solomon."

"I have video footage tying you to me just before Scully was murdered. It looks like we spoke, although I don't remember what was said."

Gray's evidence was thin, circumstantial at best. But Alice was a pious woman, and he was gambling on her conscience getting the best of her.

"And if we go back and look at footage of Tanya's last minutes on earth, I bet we'll find you there too."

"You've been such a disappointment," she said eventually. "To me, to Kate, to your children, to God."

"More of a disappointment than Reverend Hill?"

Alice looked at him. "I came into the station to tell you. To confess all. You took a long time. Too long. I changed my mind and left. Then you met her. On the harbour arm." When he and Tanya had drunk coffee beside the shell lady. So Alice had been his visitor at the station that day, not Tanya.

"Tell me."

Alice nodded. There seemed no reluctance on her behalf to speak. "You know I act in an administrative role for the church. David had always said he was pretty useless when it came to anything computer-orientated. I did people's books when I was younger, before my husband came home from the war and we had children. So, I offered to help.

"David was all too happy to accept. I taught myself how to use a computer. Quite something for a person of my age, I can tell you. I was going through some files and I found them..." Alice shuddered, unable to verbalise what was in her memory.

Gray let her pause, to expunge the memory before he asked, "What?"

"Pictures of children. Horrible, disgusting pictures. Some of the acts being committed, I couldn't believe my eyes." Her hand flew to her chest at the memory. "As I clicked through I felt someone behind me. I turned around and there he was, David, standing in the doorway, frozen in shock, eyes on the screen. He started to protest his innocence, said he was investigating child abuse, building up evidence, not perpetrating it. I left the house as quickly as I could. I wasn't able to look at him. He made me sick to my stomach.

"I wandered home. It's only a few minutes away, but it took me an hour. I don't know what happened in between. All the time I was thinking about what I'd seen. I felt so betrayed. The church, it's been my life, and David took it all away from me in those few seconds. So I decided to take his.

"I went upstairs, got the revolver, put it in my handbag and returned in my car."

"What revolver?" interrupted Gray.

"Art's."

"A drawing?"

"Art was my husband! God rest him." Alice made the sign of the cross on her chest.

"Why did he have a gun?"

"I didn't think to ask him. He was an American GI. Why wouldn't he have a gun? Besides, don't all Americans own at least one gun? Anyway, I found David kneeling at the altar, begging forgiveness of God! As if he could be exonerated from such vile acts! He should burn in Hell. So I shot him like the animal he was."

"Where?"

"In the head first. He was clearly dead. I couldn't help putting one more into his body, just to be sure. Men like him shouldn't exist on this earth."

"What about the computer?"

"I locked up the church so no one would find David's body until I was ready. I sat in his study and forced myself to look at everything. It took me all night. Worse still, I found another. A man called Scully. Abusing the weak and the powerless. It was disgusting."

"You should have brought this to the police."

"I tried. But you wouldn't give me the time of day, you just brushed past me. And Scully, he hid in plain sight, reporting on a child abuse story when he was part of it."

"Pointing the finger of suspicion elsewhere?"

"Yes, and you fools fell for it."

"None of this is my fault."

"Like Kate and Tom weren't your fault?"

Gray spoke through gritted teeth. "Don't bring my family into this."

"You have no family, Solomon."

"That makes two of us."

Alice nodded her head once at Gray in acceptance of his barb. "But I have God. Where was I? Oh yes, eventually I surmised it was God's test. Much like the way he challenged Job's loyalty through famine, loss, and death. It was God's way of seeing if I still believed. The church is out of favour, but I am still His willing servant."

Gray attempted to steer her back on track. "Where's the computer now?"

"In the boot of my car. It couldn't stay in the vicarage."

"What about Tanya?"

"Your slut?"

Gray almost slapped Alice.

"You remember I said David saw you as his mission? Well, that wasn't quite true. You were *mine*. I wanted to bring you back. She was leading you astray. And you entered the sanctity of union with Kate."

"Kate's dead."

"So's Art, but I still wear his ring." Alice showed Gray the gold band. "It's a commitment for life, both your lives."

"Kate's dead," repeated Gray.

"I know, I was there."

"You were there? What do you mean? She was alone when she died."

"You'll have to wait for that revelation, Solomon. Because of your commitment to Kate I kept a close eye on you, with your woman. When you committed your act of adultery with that whore, I felt so let down. You betrayed my best friend. And your whore wore scarlet, the very colour of sin. It was a sign. I followed her onto the beach when she went down to see the rising sun. She deserved to die.

"But Art's gun wouldn't fire. The stupid harlot didn't hear the hammer fall over the waves. I couldn't forsake Kate. I continued my task at hand, and as I got close, hit her with a rock. She went down in the surf. Blood started to spread in the water. She wasn't moving. I cleared the useless bullet from the chamber, and pulled the trigger again. It fired that time."

Gray's stomach dropped, and he felt hollowed out. He had to press on, though.

"Where's the gun?"

She bent down, picked up a handbag from her feet. She stuck a hand inside, pulled an old revolver from within. A Webley.

"Here." Alice held it out for Gray to take. "Take your revenge, Solomon. Kill me."

Gray stretched out his hand. Perhaps she was right. Perhaps he should kill her. No one would blame him. Then, before he took hold of the gun, Gray caught her smile. Her expression of beatific self-satisfaction. He shook his head, pulled his hand back.

"David was telling the truth."

"What about?" Alice froze, confused by the change in direction.

"He was investigating child abuse. The reverend was blameless. You killed an innocent man."

Alice blinked. "You're lying."

"You killed an innocent man."

"I've killed before."

"Who?"

"Only when it was deserved."

"*Who?*"

"You know, Solomon. You've always known. I just did what you couldn't bring yourself to. Marriage is sacrosanct."

Gray snapped then. He made a grab for the gun. But Alice was ready for him and struck Gray on the temple with the gun butt. He fell back onto the pew, his vision blurred.

"Useless right up to the end, Solomon." Alice raised the gun, aimed it at Gray. She pulled back on the hammer, the noise loud. There was no way she could miss.

"Do it, Alice, there's nothing to live for."

"You always were a coward." Alice put the gun under her chin and, before Gray could react, pulled the trigger.

GRAY'S EARS WERE STILL ringing by the time Hamson arrived on the scene. He was spattered with Alice's blood.

"Are you all right?" asked Hamson.

"I'm alive, so that's a good start."

Briefly, Gray explained what had happened.

"There was nothing you could have done to stop her," said Hamson.

"Maybe I didn't want to."

"Keep that to yourself. Come and get your head seen to."

Gray allowed himself to be led away.

Forty Six

Smoke curled upwards in a great plume. The fire burnt fiercely, at odds with the weak sun hanging low in the sky. Gray dragged an overflowing bin bag across the garden. He watched the flames shimmer. Great pieces of grey ash wafted up in the thermals and carried over the fence across several gardens. Children were laughing, jumping to catch the fragile flakes.

He grabbed a fistful of the yellowed, curling paper. There were years of pain stored up in careful loops and curls of neat handwriting. Without a second's thought Gray tossed them onto the conflagration. It immediately caught, tinder-dry, and turned to smoke.

Gray threw handful after handful into the cleansing blaze. Although Hamson wasn't able to return any of the official case notes there was plenty of history to get rid of. He had folders full of newspaper cuttings and handwritten notes. The process would not be a fast one. And in the morning there would be a nasty black patch on the lawn. Gray didn't care. It was a start on the garden blitz.

"What's it like being famous?" a familiar voice asked.

Gray looked up. It was Pennance. He stood at the garden gate, the picture of suave in a well-cut, three-piece suit.

"I can do without all the attention, frankly." Gray had made the national papers. A death in a church and a serial killer had been big news.

"I rang the bell, but you didn't answer," said Pennance.

"I can't hear it out here. Come on and give me a hand."

Pennance did so, and for a few minutes the pair loaded the past into the consuming flames.

"Is this a social visit?"

"Not exactly. I'll be heading back to London this afternoon. I thought I should come round and say my goodbyes."

"I'm glad you did."

"And to take you somewhere."

"I'm off booze for the moment."

"That wasn't my intention. Have you got a black tie?"

OF THE THREE PEOPLE in the crematorium, only two were breathing. Gray and Pennance were seated on the front row. Buckingham had no known next of kin, no one to look out for him in life. The least the pair of them could do was ensure Buckingham made his final journey accompanied by someone who cared.

A cheap casket containing the last remains of the sixteen-year-old boy already rested on the conveyor that would transport the body into the cleansing flames.

Gray had squeezed himself into an old suit and found a half-decent white shirt, although he'd come up short in the tie department. Dark blue was the best he could do. The service was brief, delivered by the local vicar from the church next door. The crematorium was wedged between the church and a council tip, a juxtaposition Gray didn't want to explore.

Once the reading was over, the vicar shook Gray's and Pennance's hands, mumbled a few appropriate but irrelevant words and departed.

Outside, Gray said, "This is where one of us should suggest going to the pub because every interment should be accompanied by a wake. But I'm sober and you've a train to catch."

"I do have enough time for confession, though."

"Not you as well. I've had enough of those recently."

Pennance laughed. The sound suited him. "There's something I probably shouldn't have done. Actually, two things."

"Then you came to the right place. I've a list as long as your arm of stuff that would fit into that category. Go on, tell all in gory detail."

"I kept that DS of yours on the Buckingham case alongside me."

"Fowler?"

"That's him."

"Hamson will be furious."

"Which is one reason I'm telling you and not her. It's my way of apologising."

"I'll tell her once you're in London, perhaps you'll avoid her wrath then."

Pennance laughed. "What do you think of the neighbour, Ian Wells?"

"The housebound Goth? How do you know about him?"

"From the case notes, of course."

"What about him?"

"He told you he's housebound?"

"Yes. He gets away once a week with some charity. I can't remember what they're called."

"Out and About."

"That's them."

"Fowler's digging revealed that Wells actually *works* for Out and About."

"So he's not housebound?"

"No, and he claimed there was a trip out by the charity on the day of Buckingham's death too. But there wasn't. Why lie about those things?"

Gray thought for a moment. "He told me he heard his neighbours through the wall because he was in all the time. Perhaps Wells ignored the door-to-door and avoided revealing himself?"

"It's all supposition, unfortunately."

"Let's go talk to Wells, see what he has to say for himself."

Pennance shook his head. "He's yours. And you might want this." He gave Gray the photo of Buckingham which Hamson had confiscated. "From a friend."

Gray offered his hand. Pennance grinned and shook it.

"I'll be going," said Pennance.

Now there was just one more death to clear up. The one which had started it all. Gray rang for a taxi.

Forty Seven

Gray waited too long for the lift to arrive. As he did so, he removed his tie, bunched it up and shoved it into his coat pocket.

The doors stuck part way open, as usual. Inside, he pressed the button for the floor he wanted. It wasn't any quicker to rise than before, and the smell hadn't improved either.

By now the police tape was gone from outside Buckingham's flat. Somebody had probably moved in already. A family from outside the area, he'd bet, keen to get a roof over their heads, not fussed about what had happened – the past was the past, after all.

Gray knocked. Ian Wells opened the door faster than it had taken Gray to navigate five floors.

"What do you want?" asked Wells. He looked furtive, his eyes shifting constantly, barely resting on Gray.

"To talk."

"I read about you in the paper. You're not a copper anymore so no, you can't," said Wells, trying to close the door. Gray stopped him with a well-placed foot.

"I'm taking a holiday, there's a difference." Which wasn't quite true. Gray was still deciding whether to resign from the force. He pushed the door back open. Wells barely resisted.

"This is harassment. I'll report you." There was no conviction in Wells's tone. "Clear off."

"Are you sure this is how you want it to be?"

Wells folded his arms across a black T-shirt, covering the name of some band Gray had never heard of, stressed almost to ripping point by the big man's girth.

"We'll do it another way, then," said Gray and handed over the photo of Nick with the faceless man. A man of a remarkably similar build to Ian Wells. His mouth fell open, and his hands began to shake.

"You're crazy," Said Wells.

"No, Mr Wells, I'm angry. You see, my colleague has been digging into your background. DS Fowler may be an arsehole, but he's a very persistent arsehole. Keeps going when everyone else around him is caught up in other issues, seemingly larger ones. Not Fowler. He found out that there is indeed a charity called Out and About."

"So? Of course there is."

"So you're an employee, not one of its clients. Why did you lie about that?"

Wells attempted a blank expression, but struggled to keep it together. A tic developed under his right eye.

"And there was no outing on the day Nick was murdered. Why did you lie about that, Mr Wells?"

Wells said nothing.

"Good thing Fowler checked, otherwise you might have got away with it," said Gray.

"Got away with what?"

"The murder of Nick Buckingham. We found fingerprints on the glass holding down the suicide note. We checked yours. There was a match."

Wells's face was now the shade of cheap white paint. He looked defeated.

"That's you in the photo, isn't it? We can check your tattoos, see if they match this one." He pointed at the smudge on the shoulder of the man in the photo.

Wells sagged. He fell against the wall, then slid down onto his knees. "I didn't murder him," he said in a small voice, his eyes imploring. Tears spilled down Wells's cheeks.

"You flung him off the balcony!"

"No, no! I'd never do that, I loved Nick."

Gray took a gamble, said, "He didn't love you though, did he?"

"That's not true!"

"It was all about money for him."

"No!"

"You were just another punter, someone to get drugs from."

"I was more than that! He told me so."

"Which kept you coming back for more, begging him to keep you company."

"That's not how it was!"

"And what did Nick do when you told him how you felt? I bet he laughed."

Wells didn't speak. Gray pressed harder.

"That's what he did. He laughed at you, didn't he?"

"Yes, right in my face!"

"I bet that hurt you more than anything."

"Yes," said Wells, his voice a whisper now. "It hurt so much. I took him by the arm, tried to shake some sense into him. It didn't work. He laughed again, pulled away from me.

"Nick went onto the balcony to have a smoke. I followed him. I was crying like a baby. Next thing I knew there was a scream from below. Nick was gone. I'd pushed him over. I panicked. I wrote a quick suicide note, went back into my flat as quickly as I could and hid. I hid. I hid..." Wells covered up his eyes with both hands, bowed his head as if in prayer. He blew a huge breath out of his lungs and seemed to collapse into himself, suddenly much smaller. "Oh God, it's been a nightmare, living with Nick's death." Wells looked up at Gray again. "I'm glad it's all over. Thank you."

Gray thought of Tom. Of Tanya, of Buckingham, of Hill, of Alice. And Kate. All dead, all watching him. This was his job. And whatever Alice had believed, Gray didn't need saving. He could do that for himself.

Detective Sergeant Solomon Gray raised his warrant card. "Ian Wells, I am arresting you for the murder of Nick Buckingham."

Forty Eight

When Gray brought Wells in it caused a stir in the station. Carslake was first to arrive, just as Wells was being put into his cell. Carslake stood watching proceedings for a few moments, before requesting he and Gray head up to his office.

"How did you put it all together?" asked Carslake.

Gray didn't feel like talking but there were some things that had to be said. "I had a lot of help. Hamson, Pennance, and particularly Fowler."

"Fowler?"

"He was the one who found out Wells wasn't telling the truth."

"Write it up in a report and I'll see Fowler gets the credit."

"Good. Is that everything?" Gray began to rise, keen to get out.

"No. Sit back down."

Gray did so, reluctantly. He let the silence stretch. Whatever Carslake had to get off his chest Gray wasn't going to make it easy for him.

"Whatever you think, Sol, I've always had your back."

"Sure." Gray hoped Carslake picked up on the sarcasm in his tone.

"Yes. You're not the only one who never stopped looking for Tom."

"I find that hard to believe."

"Why? We were best friends. He was like a son to me."

"It felt like you'd forgotten Tom, like he was history."

"Never. He's never far from my mind. Who do you think gave Pennance the photo of Wells?"

"Hamson."

Carslake shook his head. "It was me. I took it out of the evidence folder. I put my career on the line to help you. I'd do it again if it meant we could bring Tom home."

Gray struggled to process Carslake's confession. It was totally unexpected and flew in the face of a belief Gray had built up over so long. "I don't know what to say, Jeff."

"You don't need to say anything. We're friends. Don't forget that again."

"I won't."

"Can we work together again? You and me, looking for Tom, together."

"Yes."

Carslake held out his hand. Gray took it. "You've no idea what it means to hear you say that."

"Good. Because here's the thing, Sol. I may have a new lead..."

If you enjoyed Dig Two Graves I'd greatly appreciate it if you would write a review. They really help authors like me grow and develop.

Thanks! It means a great deal.

And if you want to sign up to a periodic newsletter with information on launches, special offers etc. (no spam!) then you can do so HERE[1].

In return is a *free* book in the Konstantin series, ***Russian Roulette***, a unique and gritty crime thriller featuring an ex-KGB operative living undercover in Margate.

Now Read The Next In The Gray Series...

Burn The Evidence

About the Author

Keith Nixon is a British born writer of crime and historical fiction novels. Originally, he trained as a chemist, but Keith is now in a senior sales role for a high-tech business. Keith currently lives with his family in the North West of England.

You can connect with me on various social media platforms:

Web: http://www.keithnixon.co.uk

Twitter: @knntom[1]

Facebook: Keithnixonauthor[2]

Blog: www.keithnixon.co.uk/blog[3]

---

1.   https://twitter.com/knntom

2.   https://www.facebook.com/keithnixonauthor/

3.   http://www.keithnixon.co.uk/blog

Other Novels by Keith Nixon

The Solomon Gray Series
 Dig Two Graves
Burn The Evidence
Beg For Mercy
Bury The Bodies
The Konstantin Series
Russian Roulette
The Fix
I'm Dead Again
Dark Heart, Heavy Soul
The DI Granger Series
The Corpse Role
The Caradoc Series
The Eagle's Shadow
The Eagle's Blood

Dig Two Graves
Published by Gladius Press 2018
Copyright © Keith Nixon 2018
Second Edition

Cover design by Jim Divine.

Don't miss out!

Visit the website below and you can sign up to receive emails whenever Keith Nixon publishes a new book. There's no charge and no obligation.

https://books2read.com/r/B-A-BGNH-SBXW

BOOKS 2 READ

Connecting independent readers to independent writers.

Did you love *Dig Two Graves*? Then you should read *Burn The Evidence* by Keith Nixon!

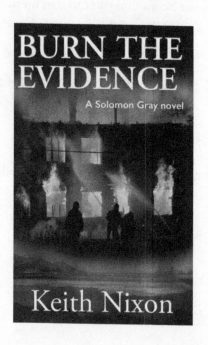

Mixing business with family can be a murderous affair ...A body washes up on the beach near Ramsgate in the South of England. For Detective Sergeant Solomon Gray, the case appears cut and dried – the drowning of an immigrant. Another victim to the sea in his desperate attempt to reach the UK.As the tidewaters recede, two more corpses surface. One appears to also be a refugee, but he's been stabbed to death. The other, Gray recognises immediately and Gray knows this means trouble. Because the corpse is the son of local business tycoon Jake Armitage, a man with a dark reputation and an ex-school friend of Gray's.A post mortem reveals ligature marks on the son's wrists and drugs in his bloodstream. All signs indicate murder. Armitage swears to track down his son's killer and avenge his death.Gray's investigation points to a deadly fire ten years prior, and soon Armitage comes under suspicion. But Gray knows what it's like to lose a child and puts aside his distrust of Armitage to help. How are the dead men connected to each other – and to the infamous fire? **It's then that Gray gets another tip. On the whereabouts of his own missing son ...**Set in the once grand town of Margate in the south of England, the now broken and depressed seaside resort becomes its own character in this dark detective thriller, perfect for fans of Ian Rankin, Stuart MacBride, and Peter James.*Burn the Evidence* is the second book in the series featuring Detective Sergeant Solomon Gray. Pick it up now to discover whether Gray can escape his past in this taut crime series.

What Others Say

"Accomplished writing from one of the best authors in the UK."**M.W. Craven**, author of the *Washington Poe* series"Keith Nixon is one hell of a writer."**Ken Bruen**, author of the *Jack Taylor* series"... deeply emotional, a dark rollercoaster ride."**Ed James**, author of bestselling *DI Fenchurch* series"Keith Nixon's latest Solomon Gray murder mystery pushes all the hot button issues of a traumatised post-Brexit UK in this dark tale of loss, revenge and redemption. Flawed and floored by personal tragedy, DS Solomon Gray is ready to take his place alongside DS Logan McRae, DS Roy Grace and DCI John Luther. Modern jet-black Brit Noir at its best."**Tim Baker**, CWA shortlisted author of *Fever City*

What Readers Say

"I'm left with a thirst which can only be quenched by reading the next in the series.""It's not often I give 5* but I did with this one.""A cracking multi-level read.""Another great thriller.""Loving this series. Sol is magnificent.""Thoroughly enjoyable, I can't wait for the next episode!""A compelling murder mystery with a multilayered and engaging new hero. Great read."**Mason Cross**, author of the *Carter Blake* thriller series"A dark, uncompromising tale of loss, murder, and revenge. Glorious noir, which takes the police procedural elements and gives them new life. I can't wait to read the next step in Solomon Gray's journey for answers ..."**Luca Veste**, author of the *Murphy and Rossi* crime series

Also by Keith Nixon

Caradoc
The Eagle's Shadow

Detective Solomon Gray
Dig Two Graves
Burn The Evidence
Beg For Mercy
Bury The Bodies

DI Granger
The Corpse Role

Konstantin
Russian Roulette
The Fix
I'm Dead Again

Dark Heart, Heavy Soul

Standalone
The Solomon Gray Series: Books 1 to 4: Gripping Police
Thrillers With A Difference

About the Publisher

Gladius Press is a small, yet highly innovative publisher of crime, humour and historical fiction novels based in Manchester in the UK.

Made in the USA
Las Vegas, NV
02 September 2023